PRIVATE ISLAND

M J HARDY

Copyrighted Material

Copyright © M J Hardy 2022

*M J Hardy has asserted her rights under the Copyright, Designs and Patents Act 1988
to be identified as the Author of this work.*

*This book is a work of fiction and except in the case of historical fact, any resemblance
to actual persons, living or dead, is purely coincidental.
All rights reserved. No part of this book may be reproduced or transmitted in any form
without written permission of the author, except by a reviewer who may quote brief
passages for review purposes only.*

This book uses UK spelling

PRIVATE ISLAND

Only the invited get to stay.
Only the lucky ones get to leave.

When Katrina Darlington lost everything, she turned to a stranger for help.

Desperate and grieving, she trusted the hand of friendship and travelled halfway across the world to a very private island.

Blue skies, blistering sunshine, and luxury on a scale way beyond the average person's means.

The perfect place to start again, surrounded by warm and friendly people who have your best interests at heart.

Or not!

Catalina Island is an island paradise hiding a sinister secret.

Will Katrina become just another one of its victims, and after having lost everything, discover she still has even more to lose?

When the people you trust most in the world turn out to be the ones you should have feared all along.

Desire creates lies and deception, but is having it all worth losing your humanity?

It's time to find out.

When you lose everything, the only thing left to find is yourself.

Escape with the perfect read this Summer and discover that sometimes in life fate plays no part at all.

"It is not in the stars to hold our destiny but in ourselves." — *William Shakespeare*

1

The only warmth in my life right now is the sun beating down on the back of my head as I peer into oblivion. It's strange what goes through your mind when you're living your darkest hour.

I don't even register the fact I'm all alone in the world. The only family I had are now settling into their new home.

'*Ashes to Ashes, Dust to Dust,*' are words I've heard thousands of times before, but now they are mocking me. My whole life has turned to dust along with them because now I must cope —alone.

My neighbour, Betty Adams, places a comforting hand on my arm and pats it almost absentmindedly.

I'm grateful for any show of compassion, any company even because now the world is a very frightening place.

My moment has come and as I approach the double burial, I swallow hard and blink behind my oversized glasses as I place two identical white roses in their forever home.

"I love you."

I whisper to each in turn and, for a moment, just stare into the abyss in every way possible.

The next person adds their own tribute to my parents, and I step away, vowing to return within a few hours to say a more personal goodbye.

I never got that chance because I left before they woke up on that fateful day and when the police came looking for me at college, it was to tell me they were gone. Forever.

Such a final word; so painful to hear. I can't bear the emotions that hit me like a bat in the face every time I realise that I am never going to see them again.

Death by accident. The coroner says, anyway. Driving to the supermarket and meeting a steep embankment along the way.

"We think they swerved to avoid something on the road and crashed through the barriers." The policeman said with a look of sympathy as he delivered the devastating news.

Just like that. Two lives ended and one left in grief.

"Come on, love, let's get you a nice cup of tea, or something stronger if you like."

Betty is so kind and has been a godsend this past month as I've dealt with things an eighteen-year-old girl should never have to do.

"Excuse me."

We look up and see an extremely glamorous woman standing before us with sympathy flashing from her stunning blue eyes. I don't think we've ever met, but there is something almost familiar about her.

"Excuse me for interrupting, but my name is Madelaine Covington. I was a friend of your parents."

I'm a bit confused because I don't remember ever meeting her before and it must show in my expression because she smiles kindly. "We lost touch a few years back, but when I heard of their tragic accident, I had to come and pay my respects."

"Thank you. They would have appreciated it."

The words stick in my throat because just thinking of them in the past tense is too painful and I'm surprised when she pulls a business card out of her pocket and says kindly, "Here are my contact details. Once everything settles down, please give me a call. You may be glad of a friend because, from what I know, you have no family to count on right now."

"That's very kind of you." I'm a little surprised because I wasn't expecting offers of help anytime soon and she reaches out and pats my arm in a show of compassion.

"I would love to help in any way I can. They would have wanted it this way."

She sighs heavily and looks past me across the graveyard and says almost to herself, "I can't believe I'll never see them again. Fate deals a cruel blow to the most undeserving people sometimes."

She looks back and sighs. "I must be going, but please, stay in touch. I'm here for you, Katrina."

Before I can even thank her for coming, she walks away and Betty whispers, "She was obviously way ahead of me in the creation queue. Look at that figure and did you notice her skin? Alabaster, they call it. Perfect nails, teeth, hair and she obviously doesn't shop at the chain stores like the rest of us. I hate her already."

Despite myself, I smile as Betty shakes her head, looking so envious I say with a soft, "I like you just the way you are, Betty."

She smiles and I hate seeing the tears in her eyes as she says sadly, "It's not right you being all alone. You know I'm always here for you, don't you love?"

"I know."

The other mourners file past, neighbours, friends, and people they worked with. Nobody important, not to me, anyway, and as the last one leaves, I turn back to the freshly dug grave and fight back the tears as I crouch beside the open pit. Two coffins, side by side, united in death as they were in life.

"You know Betty..." Her hand on my shoulder is comforting as I say thickly, "I'm really going to miss them."

"Me too, love, me too."

My tears fall and join my parents and I'm conscious of the gravedigger waiting to wrap them up warm for the night and so I stand and smile at Betty as bravely as I can and say in a small voice, "I think I'd like that cup of tea now."

∽

THERE IS NO WAKE. No gathering to celebrate their lives and reminisce about good times. My parents were so wrapped up in each other, they never wanted anyone else, so at least they both ended their life at the same time. Forever together. I'm glad about that at least.

It's just me and Betty, who lives next door with her three cats and many plants. She was married, but her husband left her for a woman at work and she never replaced him, preferring her own company along with her pets, who, in her words, never let me down.

I sit in her bright kitchen nursing a cup of tea and feel a certain sense of relief as I take a moment to think about how different my life is now.

"It was a beautiful service, Katrina. They would have been as proud as punch to see their little girl saying such lovely things about them, especially in grief. You did them proud."

"Thank you."

To be honest, I could barely get the words out and faltered so many times the guests for the next funeral were lining up at the door. Luckily, the priest intervened and kindly finished reading my carefully prepared script, while I desperately tried to pull myself together, but I tried at least so I think they would have been proud about that.

"Would you like a hand sorting things out? I'm considered quite good at that, you know."

"It's fine. I'm not going to rush into anything. The solicitor is coming around tomorrow to discuss the Will, so I think I'll wait until then."

Betty shakes her head and refills my mug with tea, sliding a slice of cherry cake towards me. "You should be ok; I think they paid their mortgage off years ago, and Colin was a shrewd investor. I'm guessing money will be the least of your worries."

"I hope so because I don't want to lose the house as well as..."

I falter and take a deep swig of my tea. "Anyway..."

Betty sighs. "Now the funeral is over, you can stop and think for a bit. You have the summer to work things out; maybe take some time to think about what you're going to do. I mean, you could go anywhere in the world when college finishes. Maybe book a holiday or go and stay with a friend. Get away for a bit and have a change of scene."

"Sounds good."

I smile even though it physically hurts to do so. "Thank you, Betty. You've been so kind, and I couldn't have done this without your help."

She blushes and waves her hand dismissively. "Nonsense, you don't need to thank me. It was the least I could do."

As I think about the funeral, the glamorous woman pops into my mind. "You know, Betty, my parents never told me about Madelaine. I wonder how she knew them?"

"I didn't recognise her. I would have remembered on the spot if I had. She's certainly memorable, that's for sure."

Thinking about the striking friend of my mother's, I must agree with her. She was definitely stylish and seemed rather kind, and I wonder what happened to create distance between them.

∼

AFTER SAYING GOODBYE TO BETTY, I take the short walk home and wonder how I can possibly live here alone. The house is large and feels even larger when there's just me in it. I wonder if I'll have to sell this too and lose another part of me that means so much.

The future is looking very unclear now and I just hope the solicitor's visit tomorrow is just a formality because the last thing I want to do is make any more decisions.

The first thing I do is shower and change into something more comfortable and try to distract my attention by catching up with a drama series I've been watching.

I only manage an hour because it feels so strange knowing I'm here alone and they won't be walking through the door anytime soon, telling me to clear up after myself and to put the kettle on.

Switching off the television, I wander aimlessly around the house and find myself in their bedroom. It's a familiar room but not one I frequented much, but knowing they will never sleep here again causes a sharp pain of resentment to slice through my heart. Why them? Why take the kindest, most amazing people in the world to another one with no warning? I wish it had been me. After all, what's the point of living without them?

Climbing under their duvet, I hug the pillows and sob my heart out because my parents have died and I'm so afraid.

2

The solicitor is feeling awkward. I can tell that the minute I open the door and he regards me with a nervous expression.

"Um, Miss Darlington. I'm Mr Frobisher of Hammond and Connor."

"Of course, please come in." I smile to put him at his ease and open the door. He follows me inside and we head towards the kitchen where I have made a pot of tea and thrown some biscuits on a plate with the usual doily underneath. It's the way my mother always used to receive visitors and I know she would be happy for me to continue the tradition.

He clutches his briefcase to his chest as if it's a lifeline and a feeling of dread prickles inside me.

"I'm sorry for your loss, Miss Darlington."

"Thank you and please call me Katrina."

He pushes his glasses further up his nose and nods. "Thank you, um, Katrina."

I watch as he opens his briefcase and removes a sheaf of papers and clears his throat.

"Your parents entrusted me with their last will and testament, and I hoped it would be many years before I had to present it."

He sighs heavily. "Far too soon; a terrible tragedy."

I nod because he's certainly right about that and he clears his throat.

"Anyway, as it happens, their will was very straightforward and may not make easy listening, so I must apologise about that."

That feeling of dread is now drowning me, and it must show because he says with a worried frown. "Do you have anyone who can be with you and support you during this time? I could wait until they get here."

"No."

I could get Betty, but I don't want to be a burden to her because I know this is her day for bingo and it's the one thing she loves, along with her cats, of course.

He looks down and I can tell he is hating every minute of this as he says sadly, "The will leaves their entire estate, including this house, their savings and any possessions to The Green Valley Foundation."

"Excuse me?"

I'm not sure if he's picked up the wrong paperwork because my parents have never once mentioned a foundation of any kind.

"I'm sorry, Miss Darlington, but I was with them when they made this will." He shifts awkwardly. "They were very clear that everything they own was to be left to The Green Valley Foundation and so it pains me to say, the house is no longer yours. Under the terms of the will, you have thirty days to vacate the property and are restricted from accessing any of their accounts. A hold has been placed on them and their assets frozen. As soon as they died, their estate reverted to the foundation and I will need you to sign a contract to say you will leave within the month."

I am astounded and just stare at him in disbelief as he shifts nervously in his seat and shakes his head.

"I'm so sorry, Katrina. I specifically asked if there were any dependants and they told me the estate had been signed over before you were born."

"So, I have nothing."

I can hear the tears in my voice as I face a very uncertain future and he says sorrowfully, "I'm afraid it looks that way. Are you sure there is nobody you can go to?"

"No, there's not."

Looking very disapproving, he slides the papers across the table and says with regret, "I'm sorry to ask you to sign this, but I need to do my job."

Lifting the pen, the signature line swims before my eyes, and I gulp as I hold it above the page. My fingers shake as I prepare to sign my life away and yet from somewhere, I feel a little of my fight return and I place the pen down and say, "No."

"Excuse me."

He looks surprised, and I shrug. "I'm not signing anything until I get this looked over by an impartial solicitor. Surely you can understand that, Mr Frobisher."

"Of course."

I gather the papers in my hand and say abruptly, "I'll be in touch when I'm ready to sign."

He nods and a faint smile ghosts his lips as he stretches out his hand towards me. "Thirty days, Katrina. Regardless of anything, this house needs to be vacant in thirty days, otherwise you will be evicted. Get a second opinion if you must, but I already know this document is legal and binding and there is no loophole to exploit."

He stands and looks sad on my behalf. "I wish you luck, Miss Darlington. I have a feeling you're going to need it."

He sees himself out, leaving me staring at a pile of paper that has just made a desperate situation even more so.

I have nothing. No family, no parents and now nowhere to live. I don't have any money to rent anywhere either and the only place I am heading is rock bottom.

∼

THREE HOURS later and I have read every line of their will. It's so cold, so practical and nothing like my parents, who were the warmest people I have ever known.

Disbelief turns to anger, which in turn makes me cry and every emotion inside me is taking a battering because what will I do now?

I still can't believe they left me nothing at all and so I start to turn out drawers, look in cupboards. Anywhere there could be an explanation for this.

However, despite my search, the only thing I find is a box of documents at the back of their wardrobe.

Once again, I sit on their bed and systematically go through every single one of them in the vain hope I can understand what's happening. There is no mention of The Green Valley

Foundation and with an exasperated sigh, I type it into the search engine on my phone.

It sits at the top of the search, but the details are few and far between. It appears to be a charitable foundation that distributes wealth to needy causes. There is no contact name, just a standard online form to request more details. There is no address, no phone number and very little information and I wonder why?

Turning back to the box, I rifle through it and the private photographs and letters my parents obviously treasured sit inside offering the sweetest kind of comfort.

It brings them back to me in a strange way and I read every word and stare long and hard at their pictures. When they first met, the look of love in their eyes makes me smile. There are pictures of me as a baby, family holidays, and celebrations through the years. Then it strikes me. It was always just the three of us, never anyone else. All through my life, we were a team, and I never thought it strange. Now I do because why didn't they entertain, invite friends around, or make connections with anyone outside this home? The people that used to visit were just associates they worked with. Not real friends they used to hang out with at weekends. Something just doesn't add up and so I continue my search and try desperately to look for anything that will give me a clue as to why we lived that way.

There is nothing in the box that helps and with an exasperated sigh, I lean back and cry bitter tears of frustration because where do I go from here?

Trying desperately to push aside my grief and deal with this latest bombshell, I systematically go through the house and try to discover anything that will give me answers and yet all I'm left with is the last will and testament of my parents that cuts me off and sets me adrift into a frightening world.

I don't even have any money for a solicitor, so I couldn't fight this even if I wanted to, and my only chance is to ask Betty for help. The trouble is, I know Betty struggles for money and I wouldn't put her in that awkward position, because it's money that I need the most. Then I think of Madelaine Covington and the soft look in her eyes and her kind offer of help.

Maybe she can give me the answers I need? She's all I've got left, so I drop the papers and head to my room in search of the lifeline she offered me.

As soon as I find the crisp white card, I breathe a huge sigh of relief. I'm just surprised I need this already. Thank goodness she heard of their death. Maybe she can give me some advice. I certainly need it and so as I dial the number, my fingers shake because she is my only hope.

The phone rings for a few seconds and then her soft voice answers.

"Madelaine Covington."

"Um, I'm sorry to disturb you but we met yesterday at my parent's funeral."

I can't stop my voice from shaking and she says brightly, "Of course, Katrina, how can I help?"

She sounds so warm and friendly, which is exactly what I need right now, and I feel a tiny spark of hope that she can help me out of this impossible situation.

"I'm sorry, but I could use your advice, really. Can we meet, perhaps?"

"Of course, I would be happy to help. Shall we say the coffee shop on the corner of Dunstable Street at ten am? Would that work for you?"

"I don't suppose you have any time today?"

I sound desperate and it certainly feels that way and she says with a hint of pity in her voice, "I'm sorry, darling, I have back-to-back meetings arranged all day. That's the best I can do before I leave."

"Leave?" If I sound slightly hysterical, it's because I see my last chance disappearing over the horizon with her and she sighs. "Yes, this is just a fleeting business trip, I'm afraid. I must return to America tomorrow afternoon."

She's American. I'm surprised at that because she certainly doesn't have an accent. She carries on, "It's where I live, but I work all over the world. I'm heading back to Florida for a few weeks, so I don't have much time. I'm sorry."

"That's fine, ten am will be perfect." I'm quick to grab the one opportunity I have left, and she says softly, "Super, darling, we can catch up then."

"Thank you."

She cuts the call and I count myself lucky that I caught her in time and as I stare at the last will and testament of my parents, all I feel is overwhelming sadness that it's come to this.

3

I am so nervous as I wait for Madelaine, and I was up half the night panicking about my situation. If I think about it, it's certainly helped push my grief to one side and yet I don't want to feel resentment towards my parents because I'm sure there's a perfectly good reason why they left everything to a faceless company. Even if it is a charitable organisation, my father's saying was always, 'charity begins at home' which makes this even more of a shock.

Maybe Mr Frobisher has this wrong and there's a reasonable explanation for this whole mess I'm in. Surely, they have provided for me in another way and so I chew my nails and count down the minutes because I am desperate for Madelaine to be my fairy godmother right now.

At exactly ten am the door opens, and she walks inside looking like an angel in a crisp white tailored trouser suit, with her long blonde hair piled on top of her head. She is clutching a designer handbag and I can even smell her perfume from where I'm sitting, and I don't miss the admiring glances she draws from just about every person in the small, rather crowded coffee shop.

Madelaine looks as if she belongs on the pages of Vogue and as she looks around, her bright smile reveals a perfect set of whitened veneers.

"Katrina, can I get you anything?" She calls across and nods towards the coffee and rows of cakes and pastries and I shake my head because I'm far too nervous to eat. Come to think of it, I haven't eaten anything since the slice of cherry cake Betty gave me and it must show because she takes pity on me and orders a tray of food and two creamy coffees.

"I thought you would help me with these. I hate to eat alone."

She drops into the seat opposite and smiles so kindly it brings tears to my eyes because a little of kindness goes a long way with me at the moment.

She says sympathetically, "You look as if you're struggling darling, how can I help?"

She nods her encouragement to help myself and as my hand closes around a warm chocolate croissant, my stomach sighs with relief.

Through mouthfuls of pastries and sips of coffee, I tell her everything and by the end of it, she shakes her head and looks a little angry.

"Oh dear, what a terrible thing to happen. You must be worried."

"I am because where will I go? What will I do?"

She looks thoughtful. "It's a difficult one that I don't have a ready answer to. Maybe I should think about it and get back to you."

The disappointment hits me hard because for some reason I really thought she would help, and she must notice it because she leans across and pats my hand with a comforting smile on her painted lips. "Leave it with me. Do you have the contract with you? I could ask my solicitor to cast his eye over it."

"But I have no money to..." She holds up her hand.

"I insist I will cover the bill. It's the least I can do under the circumstances."

"The circumstances?"

I'm confused, and she looks upset. "I feel bad that I wasn't here for your parents more. I worked with them both for many years and they were amazing people. I even met you a few times."

She laughs at the look on my face and says, "You were a baby, so I'll forgive you for not remembering. It was ages ago. You know, they were so proud of you. So happy you came into their world and completed it. I have never seen a mother's love quite like it and it was a beautiful sight to behold."

I watch her expression change as she looks back at the past and then she smiles, "Of course I will do all I can to help. It would be my pleasure."

My shoulders sag with relief and she smiles warmly. "I'll call you from home. It will probably take a week to get a second opinion though. Will you be ok until then?"

"I think so." To be honest, I'm feeling anything but ok because I have no money and not a lot of food in the house. Almost as if she's telepathic, she reaches for her purse and, offering me a large wad of notes, says firmly, "Take this. It will help keep you fed and watered, and I'll come up with a plan. Trust me, Katrina, I really do have your best interests at heart."

She glances at her watch and exhales sharply. "Goodness, I should go. My flight leaves in a few hours and I'm not even packed."

She stands and then says, almost as an afterthought, "Stay strong, darling. Everything will work out just perfectly. Leave it with me."

∼

This has been the longest week of my life as I wait for the phone to ring, but it never does.

I can't even concentrate on my studies, despite the fact I have an assignment due in before the summer break and the only thing I can do is try to sort out my parent's things and look for anything that could help me.

It's hard dealing with so many emotions the more practical tasks create, due to the memories that surround me all the time. Familiar items, a certain scent, and I can almost hear my mother's laughter as she enjoys one of my father's stories. They were so happy together and sometimes I felt in the way. Not that they ever made me feel like that, but it was impossible to burst the invisible bubble that wrapped around them both. We were a team. The three musketeers and now they've gone, I feel as if I'm missing my left and right arms.

One week to the day, the phone finally rings and just the sympathy in her voice tells me the news isn't good.

"Katrina, I'm sorry to take so long. I had hoped to get back to you before the week was out, but I had to rely on others to look into this for me."

"What did they say?"

I don't even have time for pleasantries and she sighs. "I'm

sorry darling, but your solicitor was right. There is nothing you can do. You wouldn't get anywhere with a challenge, and it would just cost you money you can't afford."

"So, I really have nothing."

It's a bitter pill to swallow, and she says with regret, "It appears so."

The tears prick behind my eyes and yet they won't fall because I'm in a state of shock. I never expected this. I thought there would be some ray of hope at least, but apparently not.

"Listen, darling..." Her soft voice cuts through the madness, "It's not the best plan out there, but I do have one suggestion to help you."

"Please, I'll consider anything." I sound so needy, so desperate, and she says with a hint of excitement, "I know of a place that is hiring for the summer. I believe college ends this week and you may want to earn some money."

"Yes, I would definitely be interested in that. What is it?" I feel as if I'm drowning at sea, and I spy a lifeboat in the distance and stop breathing for a moment as I wait for it to rescue me.

"It involves travelling, I'm afraid, which may be a blessing in disguise given your situation."

"I have no choice; anything is better than the streets, which is where I'm heading in three weeks' time."

"Well, it's summer work on an island off the coast of Florida. It's a live-in position and offers all your meals, a uniform and a place to stay. They will look after you in return for helping out and it will give you some thinking time, if nothing else."

My heart sinks. "But I can't afford the airfare. I'm sorry but..."

She cuts in. "I can arrange a ticket for you, call it a loan and then when you get straight, no matter how many years that takes, you can pay me back."

"You would really do that for me?"

"In your parent's memory, of course. I will take care of you."

Just knowing I have one option shakes the burden from my shoulders and I say eagerly, "I'll do it, thank you."

She almost sounds relieved. "That's great; good decision. I'll arrange your flight and email you the details. Text me your address and I'll get right on it."

"I don't know how I can ever thank you, Madelaine."

I really mean that because without this, I would be homeless.

"It's my pleasure darling. I am happy to help." Her soft, kind voice is just what I need to hear and as she cuts the call, I'm left with a hopeful feeling that not everything is lost. At least for the summer, I will have a roof over my head and a place to think. Maybe I can apply for benefits and continue college by renting a small room. My wages will be useful to save as a deposit and it's a start I suppose.

At least I have a plan now and probably don't have long to prepare for that, so I start immediately and begin searching for my passport and everything I need to travel abroad.

4

It was so hard saying goodbye to Betty, and it was painful walking out of my family home, knowing I would never return. I was only given a week to prepare, and I used it wisely. Betty helped and drove me to a car boot sale on Sunday and we sold as much as we could to raise some money. My parent's clothes, personal possessions and anything I could get some money for, was sold out of the boot of a car in a terrible act of desperation. I know they weren't mine to sell, but the thought of this foundation rifling through their things made me angry even thinking about it.

Betty helped me every day, and we systematically sorted every room and the only things I kept were personal photographs. Betty promised to store them for me until I could get straight and invited me to stay with her when I returned from Florida to continue my education. I don't know what I would have done without her these past few weeks, and saying goodbye caused a fresh bout of tears to drench my face. Puffy eyes are all the rage right now, at least that's what I tell myself because mine are now permanently that way.

She drove me to the airport, and we bid one another a tearful farewell and as I checked in, I hoped I wasn't going to regret this decision. I tried to google islands off the coast of Florida, but it appears to be a private island with very little details on it.

Madelaine sent my ticket along with instructions and it couldn't have been any easier. I'm to hop on a flight to Miami, where a car will take me to Naples. Then I must wait in the coffee shop by the dock where a boat will arrive to take me to the private island.

It all sounds simple enough, but I've never travelled alone and certainly not as far, so it's with a great deal of trepidation mixed with some excitement that I touch down in Miami and prepare for hopefully a life changing experience.

∾

Madelaine certainly knows how to organise, and I am met on arrival by a man holding up a sign with my name on it.

As I head towards him, he nods respectfully.

"Miss Darlington."

"Yes."

"Welcome to Miami. I'm Joe, your driver."

He reaches for my case and as we walk from the terminal, it feels as if this is happening to somebody else.

The heat hits me as soon as we exit the building and warms my spirit just as much as my body.

"Ever been to Florida before?" Joe says cheerily.

"No, never."

"It's a special place. You'll love it."

"I'm sure." I'm feeling quite nervous as we walk towards a smart minivan, and I watch as he opens the back and places my case inside.

Then he holds open the rear passenger door and says pleasantly, "You'd better make yourself comfortable. We have quite a drive."

It feels as if I've been travelling for days instead of several hours and it doesn't take long before I drift off to sleep.

When I wake, it takes a moment to remember where I am and then it hits me again–I'm all alone.

I wonder if I will ever recover from this because it's not getting any easier as the days go by. It will be a month tomorrow when the accident claimed the lives of the most important people in my world and now I'm here in Florida to work for the summer. I don't even know where I'm going, and I was so desperate, I just trusted a stranger and came here, anyway.

I look with interest at the passing scenery and love how the sun shines brightly and I see the clear crystal water of the Gulf of Mexico glittering outside. It feels as if I'm on the edge of the world looking in and for a moment, I allow myself to let go of the past and look with interest at my future. Clear skies, without a cloud in sight. Brilliant sunshine high in the sky, casting its rays across the sparkling water, making everything appear magical. I'm not used to this. I'm used to dull days and cold nights. Even summer in England is hit and miss sometimes and I can see why Florida is called the Sunshine State because this place is paradise.

My driver doesn't say much and so I'm left with my thoughts, which scare me sometimes. If I dwell too much on the future, it fills me with fear. I need to think of the way forward because I want to finish my education and study to be a doctor. We spoke about it often enough and my parents supported me one hundred per cent and I know they would be encouraging me now. Pretending this isn't happening to me isn't an option because I'm in survival mode and need to think of a new life plan because the old one has crashed and burned–literally.

If I think about that day, it's with the hope it was quick. A moment of distraction that had devastating consequences. I expect an animal ran into the road and my father lost control that he never got back. I don't like thinking of the car toppling off the cliff into the valley below before it burst into flames. They must have been terrified, and that's what hurts the most. At that moment, there was nothing they could do because fate decided their time was up.

"Soon be there."

The slow drawl of my driver grabs my attention and I look with interest at yet another amazing scene out of the window.

Naples, Florida, appears to be a beautiful place. Large houses and wide roads all set in view of the clear, sparkling ocean.

"Is the island far?" I'm curious, and Joe shakes his head. "Twenty minutes by boat. You'll soon be there."

I feel relieved about that because I'm desperate to change and grab some sleep if I can, although I am nervous about meeting new people.

Joe stops by a pleasant looking coffee shop overlooking the marina and says, "End of the road." He jumps from the car and opens my door, and a burst of heat hits me as I step outside. It's as if I left all my problems back in England and I feel a lightness to my spirit that wasn't there before.

He hands me my case and nods towards the coffee shop.

"Wait in there. You may want to grab a coffee because I think you've got a while before the boat arrives."

"How will I know which boat it is?" I'm a little anxious about that and he grins. "Don't you worry, honey, they'll find you."

I'm not sure if I should pay him and reach for my purse and he shakes his head with a grin. "All paid. Keep your dollars for the coffee."

"Oh, thank you so much." I feel bad that everything is being done for me by strangers I never heard of until now. Ordinarily I would be worried about that, but after the month I've had nothing surprises me now.

Joe heads back to his cab and leaves me alone in a strange country in a place I have never even heard of until now. If someone asked, I would probably have said Naples was in Italy. That was the only place I knew, but Naples, Florida, is a spectacular vision of happiness, and I am looking forward to seeing what it has to offer.

The coffee shop is half empty and I feel the curiosity of my fellow customers as I wheel my case inside and look for a table. The woman behind the counter shouts, "Candy! Customer!" I look up and see a young girl heading my way with a smile and she says, slightly breathlessly, "Sorry, I was out the back. Do you need a table for one?"

"Yes – please." I smile nervously and she cocks her head towards my case and says with interest, "Just arrived; where are you heading?"

She shows me to a booth near the window and I smile. "An island not far from here. I don't have the name, but apparently a boat will come to take me there."

"I expect you're talking about private island."

"Is that its name?"

I'm a little surprised at that and she laughs. "It's what the locals call it. Nobody really knows its name. In fact, I doubt it's even got one."

"Surely it has a name." I feel a lot more nervous now as she shrugs.

"Well, if you find out, let me know."

She looks around and says quietly, "The thing is, nobody ever comes back to tell us the name."

"What do you mean?" Now I'm confused and she sighs. "Plenty of people turn up here with their cases waiting for the boat to private island, but we never see them again."

"Maybe they go straight to the airport." I'm not sure why I'm making excuses for them, and she shrugs.

"Maybe."

She doesn't look as if she believes me, and I feel a tiny doubt creeping into my mind as I contemplate the journey I'm about to make. Is it safe? Looking at the expression on Candy's face, I'm not so sure and she says cheerily, "Well, you're here now, so what can I get you?"

"Just a coffee, please." I would love to order something else, but I'm so worried about money and need to save as much of it as possible.

"Coming right up."

She turns and heads off at a brisk pace, leaving me worrying about what I've let myself in for. If the locals don't even know the island's name, then that concerns me–a lot.

It must be thirty minutes later the door opens and I see a man smartly dressed in white shorts and a navy open-necked shirt head inside. I take a moment to appreciate how stylish he looks. He can't be much older than me and appears to have none of the worry attached that I now live with as he scans the room, his eyes resting on me with a spark of interest flaring in his dark brown eyes. His hair is blonde and close cut and he smiles as he sees me openly staring and heads across towards me.

"Hey, you must be Katrina."

His easy manner and open, honest face relaxes me a little and I smile. "Yes, I'm sorry, I didn't catch your name."

"It's Nathan, Nate for short. What about you? Can I call you Kat?"

His infectious grin makes me smile. "If you like."

It doesn't matter to me, but my parents hated it when my friends called me Kat because they always said I had such a pretty name and should be proud of it.

He nods towards my suitcase. "Let me help you with that. I'm here to collect you and take you to paradise."

He tosses some dollars on the table and winks. "Coffees on me. Come on, let's get you settled into your new home."

Candy waves as we leave, and I follow Nate outside and towards a white speedboat tethered to a cleat on the dock.

I watch as he jumps inside and stows my case securely before offering me his hand.

I feel a little embarrassed as I take it and allow him to help me onboard and his cheerful smile and slightly suggestive wink makes my heart race a little faster because quite honestly, Nate is the best-looking guy I have ever laid eyes on and I am more than happy to follow him wherever he likes.

5

We set off, and it feels as if the wind is pushing all my troubles away. For the first time since the accident, I feel as if a heavy cloud has lifted, and I can finally breathe again. Nate handles the boat like an expert, and I enjoy watching him skilfully manoeuvre us out of the dock and skim the waves, leading us out to the open sea.

"Hey, Katrina..." He shouts above the roar of the waves, "Settle back and relax. I'm guessing you've had a long journey and could use some rest."

"Is it far?"

I'm curious about our destination, and he grins. "Not too far, about twenty minutes, but worth every wave we ride because I'm betting you'll fall in love with our little piece of paradise."

"I didn't catch its name." I shout to get my voice heard above the roar of the engines and the slapping of the waves against the bow.

Nate laughs. "We just call it home and I'm hoping you will too."

He looks so open, friendly and seriously bad for my heart and I'm thinking that a home with him in it can't be bad at all, so I smile slightly flirtatiously and nod. "It sounds good, especially to someone without a home right now."

He says with concern, "I heard. It must have been tough."

"What have you heard?" I'm curious, and he shrugs, shouting against the noise from the engine. "That you've suffered a terrible loss and have no place else to go. Madelaine told us to help you out and give you some thinking time."

I'm keen to hear what he knows about Madelaine and shout, "Does Madelaine live here?"

"She visits."

He smiles, and it feels as if the sun shines a little brighter because Nate's smile could melt an iceberg. "We'll talk later. It's difficult right now. Just enjoy the ride; we'll soon be there."

He increases the speed, and it takes all my strength just to hold on and as I look out to sea, I try to catch a glimpse of my new summer home.

I wonder if I'll be working with Nate. I certainly hope so, and as I feel the spray cooling my heated skin, I have a very good feeling about this place they call home.

As he said, it's about fifteen minutes later when I see land and peer a little closer.

"Is that it?" I shout above the engine, and he nods. "It sure is. Soon be there."

The excitement builds as I contemplate my new destination and I look with interest as the small speck of land on the horizon gets a lot bigger the closer we get.

In fact, the more I stare, the more I fall in love with a place that appears to be fresh out of a storybook. Crystal blue waters and bright blue skies frame a jewel in the ocean. White sandy beaches outline the land, and I see gentle undulating hills that reach to the heavens. A headland juts out into the ocean and Nate points and says loudly, "That's the way in. The cove provides shelter from the elements and protects the boat. It's the only place to land on the island."

I'm not sure how big this place is, but it looks absolutely huge to me and as we draw closer, I look with interest as the sea gives way to what appears to be the most amazing resort. White buildings shine like beacons in the middle of the ocean, and lush greenery almost hides them from view. A wooden jetty stretches out and as Nate slows his speed, I look with interest at the place we're heading.

"It looks amazing."

He nods with a proud smile on his face. "I love it here. To be honest, you would struggle to find a more perfect place in the world. I really hope you decide to stay."

"Well, I'm here for the summer, although I don't know what I'm expected to do in return for my bed and board."

He smiles. "Settle in and become one of the family like the rest of us, I guess. Look after our guests and make them feel welcome."

"So, it's a hotel then?"

I'm still confused, and he laughs out loud. "Man, you don't even know where you're going, do you? I must say, Katrina, I'm impressed."

"With what?"

"Your bravery. I've got to hand it to you, I don't think I'd be as brave."

"I didn't have much choice."

I feel a little of the bitterness return because how is this even happening in the first place and Nate obviously sees my expression change because he smiles with a look of concern. "Hey, baby, chase away those demons and open your mind. Catalina Island is the only thing you need to think of right now and how amazing this summer is going to be."

"Catalina Island. It does have a name then."

"Sure, we just don't advertise the fact."

"Then how do people know to come here?"

"It's by private invite only."

"How does that work?"

Nate laughs. "I don't know if I'm honest. Madelaine runs that side of things. She sells our package and the guests come calling. Most of the time, they stay for a couple of weeks and leave refreshed and happy and that's all that concerns us. How they find us is not important, just that their visit is the best experience of their lives."

"So, what's your job on the island?" I'm keen to know more, and Nate smiles. "General dogsbody, I think it's called. I man the boat, help out with the water sports and occasionally serve in the bar. I organise activities and carry the suitcases."

"How long have you been here?"

He just laughs out loud as he expertly manoeuvres the boat alongside the jetty. "So many questions, Kat. Maybe we can discuss them over a drink later. I'm keen to get to know you."

Wow, I'm a little taken aback at the apparent interest in his eyes and can't believe my luck. A tropical paradise and a man who is looking at me as if I'm the best thing that's ever happened to him. Madelaine must have been sent from God because I couldn't have imagined this amazing outcome to a very serious problem, and I am so happy I called and asked her for help.

Nate jumps from the boat with the line in his hand and winks as he tethers us to a ring on the side and then leans in and grabs my hand. I'm a little in shock as it closes around mine and he says, "Allow me to help you from the boat. It can be a little choppy."

He nods towards my case. "I'll fetch that later. My first priority is to settle you in."

It feels strange taking his hand and as I step onto the wooden jetty, I feel the sun beating down on my head and sigh with pleasure. I feel so good about things when I should be feeling decidedly worried. It's as if the air here soothes all your troubles away and stows them away for you to pick up when you leave.

As we walk along the jetty towards a white sandy beach, I feel the excitement building. It's like living in a fantastic dream that I don't want to wake up from, and I look around with interest at the place I'll call home for the next six weeks.

"Who do I need to see?" I'm now thinking more practically, and Nate smiles. "Chester Monroe. He's the island manager and assigns the roles. I'll take you to reception and they'll let him know you've arrived."

"Is he nice?"

I feel a little worried now I'm here, and Nate rolls his eyes. "Sometimes."

He laughs, and it strikes me how open he is. It's as if he doesn't have a worry in the world and I'm interested in learning more about him. "Where are you from?"

"North Carolina." He sighs. "Like you, I suddenly found myself alone and on a difficult journey, so if you need someone to listen, I'm your man."

His words remind me why I'm here in the first place and the sudden pain that brings is difficult to deal with.

Pushing it away for another time, I focus on where I'm going instead.

Catalina Island looks like a picture postcard, and I am keen to explore. The beach looks as if we are the first people to tread on it and I have never seen one looking so perfect, almost as if it's as if it's never been walked on.

We reach a path that appears freshly laid and I smile with delight at the beautiful bushes, blooming with tropical flowers that scent the air with their sweet perfume. The only sound is the call of a solitary bird overhead, and I sigh with delight. I can't believe I'm here at all and with such good company, and I really hope I'll see a lot more of Nate during my time here.

We head towards the white building and as it gets closer, I appreciate the interior. The sides are open to the elements and the white marble floor shines as if newly polished. Huge urns contain more flowering plants, and the gentle trickle of water can be heard from a large fountain in the lobby area.

Comfortable seating invites the weary traveller to rest awhile and the coolness of the interior is a welcome relief from the intensity of the sun outside.

Nate directs me to one of the comfy seats and as I sink wearily into it, a woman appears holding a tray.

"Welcome, Katrina. We are so happy you made it."

"Um, thanks." I look at the beaming girl with interest, noting she doesn't look much older than me and she offers me a small towel from her tray. "Here, take a cool cloth to wipe away the heat of the day and sip a deliciously refreshing cocktail to revive you."

She hands me a brightly coloured drink and I eagerly accept it because I am suddenly extremely thirsty.

Nate says, "I'll let them know you're here. Then I'll fetch

your bag and take it to your room. Remember, any questions I'm always here for you, just ask someone and they'll come and find me."

He winks and heads off and I feel the loss of his company already and I note the girl's eyes follow him with a slight smile on her face. "Is he your boyfriend?" I'm not sure why I even say that and feel my face burn with embarrassment as she laughs softly. "Goodness, no. Nate is just a good friend."

I look at her keenly because I hope to God he's single, at least for the next six weeks, because I have enjoyed his company and am keen to spend more time with him.

She sighs and steps back. "Duty calls." She smiles. "If you wait here, Mr Monroe will come and welcome you personally."

I watch her walk away and feel a little on edge. I wonder if I'll be interviewed for whatever this position is and I'm not sure how I feel about that. I mean, I've had interviews before, for my job in the coffee shop in town and college, but this feels important somehow and I hope I measure up because if I'm not considered suitable, I don't know what I'll do.

Trying to distract my attention, I reach for my phone and decide to text Betty and let her know I've arrived safely.

However, there doesn't appear to be a signal and with a sigh of exasperation, I switch to Wi-Fi and look for the available ones and am surprised to find nothing at all. Not even a suggestion, which surprises me. Surely they have internet on Catalina Island. What sort of resort is this?

I must look confused because the next thing I hear is a deep voice saying with amusement, "You'll get used to it."

Looking up, I see an extremely smart man watching me with a slight smile on his face and a spark in his eyes. He looks to be in his forties and is wearing smart white chinos and a navy polo shirt. He has deck shoes on his feet and mirrored shades perched on his head and his eyes twinkle as he looks at me, a welcoming smile on his sun kissed face.

"You must be Katrina. We've been expecting you."

He offers me his hand as I jump up and say quickly, "Yes, I'm pleased to meet you..."

"Chester." His hand closes around mine in a firm grip and shakes it hard, and then he pulls back and looks at me with interest.

"So, I understand you need a job, well you've come to the right place."

"I have?"

It certainly feels that way and he cocks his head to the side, almost as if he's judging every part of me. I'm not sure how I feel about that and am glad when he says, "Follow me. I'll show you around and we can discuss your position here."

To be honest, I'm dying to explore this place a lot more, so I nod enthusiastically. "I would like that. Thank you."

As I follow him, it all looks perfectly normal, and I feel happy to be here.

Maybe my luck is about to change. I hope so because I could certainly use some good luck and maybe Catalina Island is just the place to find it.

6

Chester Monroe moves through the resort as if he personally knows every inch of it. He is a commanding presence, and I am mesmerised by him. I don't think I've ever met a man as assured as he is and I'm a little in awe of him, really. He looks to be in his late forties with dark hair showing no signs of greying just yet. He is tanned and obviously likes to work out and he is immaculate in his appearance, much like Nate and the kind girl who welcomed me.

However, for now it's just the two of us, which surprises me a little because we appear to be the only ones here, which strikes me as odd, especially in the reception area where I imagine it's usually busy with guests.

We move towards another entrance and as we head out into the sunshine, Chester removes his shades and covers his eyes and smiles.

"You must have many questions, but for now I'll give you the guided tour. We've just left the reception area where the guests check in. That will be important to you because I'm hoping you will take up the vacant position behind the desk."

"A receptionist?"

I'm amazed, and he nods. "Yes, Darcey left last week, so it was good timing. We need someone to check the guests in and answer their questions. Have you ever worked reception before?"

"No." I feel my heart drop because I really like the sound of that role and maybe he will re-think his decision. Happily though, he shrugs. "You'll soon get the hang of it. It's pretty straightforward, really."

"Have you many guests?"

I'm asking because we appear to be the only ones around and he nods. "We currently have about twelve. Some will be in their private suites that all come equipped with a pool and hot tub. Others will be in the spa or touring the island. We don't have a huge capacity which is part of the appeal. A private island getaway for the super-rich, with none of the distractions most resorts offer."

The super-rich! Wow, I'm impressed, and he carries on walking, pointing to a building in the distance that looks like a small bungalow.

"That's the spa building. We have most services on offer that are complimentary to our guests. In fact, everything is, and they just pay the one-off fee for coming here. Money is an inconvenience they can do without on Catalina, and we strive to make their stay here extremely memorable."

He points to a building on the other side of the path. "That's the fitness centre. There's a gym and classes available to suit most people's levels. Our personal trainer is Sven. He came from Norway a few years ago and lives with Katie, who works in the spa."

"Did they meet here?"

I'm interested to know, and he nods. "Yes, we're a small family on this island and it's natural to form attachments."

We reach a more open space, and he says with obvious pride. "Let me show you one of our more basic apartments. It sleeps two and is the smallest one on the island."

He pushes open the door and as we head inside, I am blown away by the opulence of his most basic room.

Marble tiles provide a welcome cool path in a room fit for a king. Modern, light and airy, it oozes wealth, from the smart polished furniture to the amazing art on the walls. We have walked into what appears to be a small sitting room where double doors lead out into a space that takes my breath away. A glistening pool sparkles in the sunlight and is furnished by white comfortable day beds that are surrounded by sheer white curtains. They easily house two people, and there are three of them. A swinging seat overlooks the ocean and I see a hot tub bubbling close by with what appears to be a built-in ice bucket on the side. All around are amazing flowers and manicured lawns and I could die happy in a place like this.

Chester says proudly, "Our guests can be as private as they like. They don't have to see a soul if they don't want to, and every room has a butler service where they can order their own preferred meals or drinks from the comfort of their day bed. Each villa is given an iPad where they just have to place an order and it's delivered to their room. We can also arrange private dining on the beach with a musician to serenade them and they have the services of a guide to show them around the island, or enjoy a trip to the mainland should they wish to explore. We want their stay here to be second to none and many leave with a very satisfied smile on their face. Customer service is paramount here and I am sure you will fit into the role like a second skin."

We head inside and he leads me into the biggest bedroom I have ever seen. The bed alone looks like a small town and all around me is luxury I never knew existed in the real world. The comfortable bed is calling to me like a long-lost friend and I feel so weary as I struggle to maintain a polite smile on my face.

When I see the bathroom, I almost swoon because I fall in love on the spot. This room is bigger than my bedroom at home and has a separate walk-in shower that looks brand new. Polished chrome and marble flooring make the room sparkle with cleanliness and the complimentary lotions and white fluffy towels, make me long to indulge in a good long bubble filled soak in the roll top bath that overlooks the ocean.

"We have three rooms similar to this one, all different in decor but roughly the same size. We also have three villas on the other side of the resort that are substantially bigger, and they sit on stilts in the ocean. They are for our guests who like a more natural experience where they can watch the ocean through a glass floor that runs the entirety of the space. They also have a private decking area where they can relax with nobody around them to disturb their solitude."

"How many guests can you accommodate at any one time?"

I have so many questions that I need to ask, and he smiles. "Fourteen. We also have a penthouse above the main building. We keep it very selective and it's unusual for us to be full. Currently, we have four couples staying, so you can ease into the job before it gets busy."

I'm wondering how much this place costs because it surely

needs the super-rich to keep it going and I wonder if I should ask.

Deciding it would be strange not to question the big boss, I say quickly, "How much does it cost to stay here?"

He doesn't hesitate. "A lot of money, Katrina, and it would be in bad taste to divulge the amount. Just know the people who pay to come here can afford it and it's taken care of before they even arrive. They don't have to worry about anything other than having a good time and enjoying the lifestyle we can provide for however long they are here."

"How many staff work here?" I'm now feeling confident to ask as many questions as necessary.

"Enough to make the guests stay extremely comfortable. We are a family here, Katrina, and work with only one common goal. To make Catalina the best experience of our guests' lives and to make their dreams come true."

He smiles, and it's impossible not to be drawn into this bubble of happiness he has created here, and I smile happily. "It all sounds and looks amazing and I'm guessing nobody leaves here without a huge smile on their face."

He obviously approves because his easy smile makes me relax. "I knew you'd love it. Everyone does and so the next thing is to show you where you'll be staying. I expect you are keen to settle in."

Now I'm even more interested and hope it's as gorgeous as the rooms he showed me and we head back to the reception area, passing a huge natural swimming pool with a diving platform crafted from what appears to be natural rock. There is also a charming veranda overlooking the ocean and a nearby beach bar that appears deserted. In fact, it feels a little eerie and I say nervously, "It's very quiet. Where is everyone?"

"The staff are making sure the guests are ok and are only needed when required. When they aren't, many enjoy alone time, use the staff gym or catch a movie. Some help prepare the food for the chef and others take a turn cleaning. We all pitch in here and do what's required. Like I said, we're one big happy family."

Once again, we reach the reception and I look at it a little differently now I know it's my new home. From what Chester says, it's not that busy and I wonder if I'll be bored. The pleasant girl heads our way and Chester smiles. "Katie, please show Katrina to her room and make sure she has everything she needs."

"Yes, sir."

She nods respectfully and smiles. "Come with me. I'll help you settle in."

As we walk away from Chester Monroe, I feel his eyes burning into my back and feel a prickle of worry inside. I really hope I shape up because now I'm here, I don't want to give them any reason to send me back to England because if I never had to leave, I would die happy.

7

Katie is very open and friendly, and I find myself relaxing around her. She shows me to a lovely room in a block of four and explains how things work.

"This is your room, Katrina. It was Darcey's, and it feels strange without her here."

"Was she here long?"

"About a year."

"Why did she leave?" Quite frankly, I can't imagine anyone actually choosing to leave this place and she sighs. "Circumstances took over, and she had to go. It's a shame though. I really thought she'd last longer."

She points to the view and says with pride. "This is your office, Katrina, and who wouldn't be happy about that?"

We wander out onto a balcony overlooking another part of the island and, like the ones I've seen already, this is no different. It all feels so manicured, perfection really and as if nothing bad ever happens on Catalina Island.

The room itself is clean, comfortable and fairly large, and consists of a small living area overlooking the ocean. Off which is a pleasant bedroom, also with floor length doors leading out onto the balcony that runs the length of it. A separate bathroom is just as luxurious as the guest rooms, with a walk-in shower and roll top bath overlooking the ocean. In fact, every window looks out on paradise and I long to soak up the sun on the sun lounger that is calling my name and Katie smiles. "I'll let you settle in. Nate left your case by the door so you can just unpack and relax for the afternoon. Chester told me to come and fetch you later to dine with the rest of the staff, so take advantage of the peace and quiet while you can because they're a friendly lot who won't leave you alone for a minute if you let them."

I say with interest, "Where are you from?"

I'm curious because I don't recognise her accent. "A little town in Texas where I lived all my life until this job became available."

"How did you know?" I'm interested to see how she found out about it.

"It came at just the right time. Like you, I needed a place to stay. My parents moved overseas and left me behind."

"Did you mind?" I'm amazed and she shrugs. "I did at the time, but when Madelaine told me about this place, I couldn't have been happier."

"How do you know her?"

She smiles. "She's a friend of my parents. They asked her to help me out and I'm glad they did because now I've met Sven, and everything is good in my life."

She sighs and says with a small smile. "Maybe you will find happiness here, Katrina. I hope so."

I don't reply and she turns and heads to the door with a cheery, "I'll come and get you at seven. Enjoy settling in."

Once the door closes behind her, I look around in disbelief. How has this happened? This place is so amazing. Luxury on a scale I have never imagined, and I am calling it home for the next six weeks. It feels too good to be true and as I fetch my case and begin to unpack, I congratulate myself on landing on my feet.

As I open the closet, there is a white starched uniform hanging on the rail and I lift it down and study it, finding a smart shift dress with a silver logo embroidered on the front, which is obviously the one the resort uses. C and I are entwined around a palm tree, and I look with interest at more items of uniform hanging alongside it. There appear to be two of everything. Two dresses, two white cardigans, and some smart white canvas shoes. Everything appears to be in my correct size, which doesn't even strike me as weird. One size must fit all around here and I'm glad of the uniform because I don't own anything smart enough to stand behind the reception desk.

However, all of that can wait because the only thing I want to do now is to strip off my travelling clothes and soak in the tub while overlooking the glorious ocean.

∽

ONE HOUR later and I'm feeling much better. It's obvious luxury suits me and just thinking of the cold, probably rainy day at home, it seems a million miles away, not just a few thousand.

I spend the next hour sunning myself on my balcony, allowing the sun's rays to warm my travel weary limbs while listening to the gentle lap of the waves against the shore, feeling the intense sun calming every part of me. Sighing with pleasure, I'm glad to find I love it here and can't wait to start my job. I never thought of myself as a receptionist before, but surely it can't be difficult. Maybe it will be the making of me. I certainly hope so.

My thoughts turn to my parents and the pain hits me hard. Maybe it always will, and I am sentenced to live in grief because when will this end? I can't possibly imagine the horror they lived through on that fateful journey and, if anything, I hope it was quick and they didn't suffer. I was told they died instantly, but there's that little shred of doubt that creeps in when it's not wanted. Sometimes I feel them with me. Hear their soft voices in my head, comforting me and telling me that everything will be ok. Maybe that's what happens in sudden deaths. The spirits linger to make sure the people left behind are cared for. It feels that way because, knowing my mum, she would have sent Madelaine to me to pick up where she left off. I like to think so, anyway.

~

A GENTLE TAP on the door reminds me I have a terrible sense of time and I quickly jump up and wrap a towel around my near naked body. Glancing at the clock on the table beside the bed, I can see it's nearly seven already. I must have fallen asleep because the sun appears to have dipped below the horizon, leaving a pleasant balmy evening.

"Hey, Katrina, it's Katie, are you decent?"

"Give me two minutes and I will be." I giggle as I pull my maxi dress from my case and quickly kick on some flip flops and open the door with a wide smile.

I'm surprised to see Katie hand in hand with a guy who must be Sven and he looks at me with interest, wearing a huge welcoming smile on his face as Katie says proudly, "Katrina, meet Sven, my partner."

I smile, feeling a little shy, and whisper, "Hi."

"Welcome, Katrina, you will love it here." His accent is different, and he seems so open and friendly it's impossible not to like him and as I fall into step beside the besotted couple, I wonder what tonight will bring.

"I hope you got some rest because there's dancing tonight." Katie grins and I say in surprise, "For the staff as well as the guests."

Sven nods. "Yes, we all mix in together when there's a social. Probably because the guests are few and it would be an evening with no atmosphere."

"Do they mind?" I'm a little taken aback, and Katie smiles. "No, they love it. Chester likes to promote Catalina Island as a family run concern, and we are all treated as such. Don't be surprised if you dance with every person here tonight; these evenings can get a little hard on the feet, and the stamina, come to think of it."

Sven gazes adoringly at his wife, partner, I'm not sure anymore and I wish I had someone to look at me like that – just once would be nice.

Maybe it's because my parents were so guarded and kept most people out, I developed that particular skill for myself. I don't have many friends, if any, and it's a sad fact that our elderly neighbour was the only friend I had in my time of need.

We pass by amazing light strewn landscaping, the soft breeze calming my heated sunburned skin. I feel as if I'm glowing like a nuclear reactor and wouldn't advise anyone to fall asleep in the sun, or even the shade, come to think of it.

Sven and Katie, on the other hand, look glowing and not just because of their fabulous suntans. Love certainly agrees with them, and I wish I could be as happy as they obviously are.

We make our way outside, where the bar is home to several guests, all sipping cocktails and cracking open bottles of champagne. I see Nate laughing with one of the guests and don't miss the flirtatious look in her eye.

Nate looks up and waves us over and as we approach, says loudly, "Maureen, meet the newest addition to our family. Katrina arrived today all the way from England."

Maureen and her husband look up and I feel a little uncomfortable as they openly stare and I'm glad when Nate says to the bartender, "Another cocktail for our newest recruit."

I look at the guy standing behind the bar who winks and slides a brightly coloured drink my way. "Hey, pretty lady, I'm Drew. Anytime you're thirsty, come and find me. Any time you're lonely..."

"Leave her alone, Drew."

Katie rolls her eyes. "Save your flirting for when she's settled in and knows what a Romeo you are."

Drew grins with a slightly wicked look in his eye and turns to Maureen. "You don't blame me, do you Maureen?"

"No, honey, she's very pretty." Maureen winks at me as Nate rolls his eyes and heads to my side. "I'm sorry, Kat, expect a lot of this tonight."

I'm surprised when he places his hand on my elbow and guides me away from the bar. "I wanted to come and find you. Help you settle in and show you around. Not the Chester Monroe tour, either. The one that gives all our secrets away."

He laughs and I feel myself relaxing. Maybe it's the alcohol content in the cocktail or the fact that everyone is so nice, but there is nothing not to like about life on Catalina Island–so far, anyway.

As nights go, this one has to be up there as the best one of my life so far. The area soon fills up with guests and staff and everyone mixes like the most exotic cocktail. All nationalities appear to be represented and the guests are happy to mingle, as if they are part of an extremely large family.

Nate remains by my side all night, which helps as he introduces me to everyone and cracks constant jokes, making me feel as if I've been here forever.

I get chatting to a lovely couple from Switzerland who are keen to know everything about my life and I am happy to oblige. The alcohol flows freely along with the conversation, and I find myself confiding in just about anyone who will listen. It really helps to open up and talk it through and the sympathetic glances they throw my way mean a lot because it shows that they care.

We are fed via a huge barbeque, grilling all kinds of delicacies, from burgers to squid and marinated meat, that tastes like nothing I've ever experienced before. I suppose I'm so used to the normal burgers and fries from our local McDonald's, I'm surprised when the food here actually has some taste to it.

Nate is very attentive, which gives me a warm feeling inside and as the night progresses, I find myself imagining us in Katie and Sven's position. I would be the luckiest girl on the planet if I ended up with him, although I constantly remind myself that in six weeks' time, I will be boarding a flight to London and returning to college to share a room with a stranger. I was offered a place in the student accommodation and must save all my wages to pay for it. It kind of throws a dampener on the evening and Nate leans down and whispers, "Is everything ok? You've gone quiet on me?"

"It's fine." I throw him a small smile. "I'm just thinking about life after Catalina. It doesn't seem so appealing now."

He smiles broadly, "I was hoping you'd feel that way. It's only been a day and I'm already planning things we can do together."

"You are?" I'm a little taken aback by that and he shifts a little closer. "If I'm moving too fast, tell me to back off, but I know you feel it too."

"Feel what?"

"A connection."

I raise the cocktail glass to my lips and take a large gulp because what is happening here?

Then I hear a loud, "There she is and with one of my favourite people."

I look past Nate and see Chester with another guy who looks a few years older than me. Nate stands beside me and grins. 'Hey, Adam, you made it."

I look at Adam with curiosity because he is the first person I've met since stepping foot on this island that looks as if he wishes he was anywhere else.

Chester laughs out loud. "I made a point of dragging him away from the pots and pans for the night. He tried to resist, but I played the boss card." He jerks his head towards the unhappy guy and says, "Adam is one of the junior chefs. He prefers to chop vegetables rather than make friends and enjoy the facilities. Sometimes I interfere and insist he take a night off."

I smile, but Adam doesn't even look at me and Nate rolls his eyes in a very clear message. Adam is the exception to the rule here, and I wonder why he's so unhappy.

Chester's attention is distracted by one of the guests and it leaves Adam hovering near us awkwardly. Nate sighs and leans a little closer, whispering, "I'll fetch us a couple of drinks. Try your best to get rid of him. You'd have a much more enjoyable evening if you did."

He doesn't even ask Adam if he wants a drink and as he heads off, leaving me with the surly chef, I say brightly, "How long have you worked here?"

Adam sighs and, leaning closer, whispers, "Don't believe everything you see here. They paint a very attractive picture, but there's something odd about this place."

"Like what?"

I'm struggling to pinpoint what that is exactly, and he says gruffly, "There's a weird vibe on this island and I'm not sure it's a place I want to be involved with."

Nate returns, causing Adam to shut down again, and it annoys me when Nate openly yawns and stares straight at him.

"The coast is clear. You can get back to the kitchen if you like. I'll distract Chester if he comes looking for you."

The look Adam throws Nate makes me catch my breath and I almost think he's going to punch him before a pleasant looking girl stops by and places her hand on Adam's. "Hey honey, I was looking for you."

She smiles at me shyly, "I'm sorry you must think me terribly rude. I'm Chloe Eversley and you must be Katrina."

"Hi." I smile, liking the pretty girl on sight. She looks friendly and around my own age and I am keen to make at least one good friend in my life, so maybe I could begin with her.

The guys stand beside us, and the atmosphere appears a little more strained and with a sigh, Chloe throws me an apologetic smile.

"Do you mind if I borrow Adam?"

"Be my guest." Nate shrugs and I nod, feeling sympathetic towards the surly chef.

"Of course."

As they leave Chloe flashes me a brilliant smile and I watch as she leads the unhappy guy behind her and Nate exhales sharply. "I don't know why Chester bothers with him. He's so creepy and really doesn't fit in here at all."

"Is he always like that?"

"Pretty much. I think the last time I saw him smile was when Jenny was here."

"Who's Jenny?"

"One of the spa assistants she used to do mani-pedis and jump in on reception if they needed a hand."

"What happened to her?"

I'm curious to know, and he shrugs. "Packed up and left one day. Wouldn't say why and we never heard or saw from her again."

"Did she travel in your boat?"

"Yes, but she wanted to be dropped on the mainland." He shakes his head. "I never even got a word of thanks. She was an odd one for sure."

"That's a shame for Adam."

Nate nods. "He was a different person around Jenny. She brought out the best in him and most people think she found something about him she didn't like, which is why she wanted to leave so suddenly."

"Like what?"

He lowers his voice. "Rumour has it she caught him in a compromising position with one of the guests."

"Surely not."

I feel shocked about that, and Nate shrugs. "It happens sometimes."

"It does."

I look at him a little differently and he laughs. "Not me though. That kind of thing doesn't interest me. I'm all for the easy life. I mean, why compromise your job on this island for a quick fling with a cougar? Some do it to subsidise their income if you know what I mean?"

I smile but feel a little sorry for Adam. He seems nice enough but obviously struggles to fit in and if anyone knows what that feels like, it's me.

8

As evenings go, this one is shaping up to be the best one of my life. I have never felt so welcome. The guests are lovely and really interested in where I'm from, what I've done in the past and are sad for me when I tell them the reason I'm here. The staff are good fun and I've lost count of the number of cocktails that Drew has slid my way. Nate is an ever-present companion and Katie and Diana provide willing dance partners when the music plays popular tunes.

The fact I'm in paradise also helps, and I never want this night to end.

After a while, the guests drift off to their rooms and the staff begin to wind down. Sven and Katie disappear, and Drew prepares to close the bar. Diana left a while ago and Nate smiles, "Come on, I'll make sure you get back to your room in one piece."

My head is spinning and as I stumble a little, I'm grateful for the arm he offers me and as I lean against him, he laughs softly. "It appears that you had a good night, Kat. I'm glad."

"I did. It was amazing actually."

Now we're away from the bright lights and bustle of the bar, I feel a little awkward walking beside Nate because I grew more interested in him the more the night progressed. Now we're heading back to my room it feels like a proper date even though I know he's only being polite.

"I'll show you around properly tomorrow. I think you'll like it here." His deep voice sends shivers of attraction through me, and I say shyly, "I think so, too."

Maybe the alcohol is giving me more courage than usual because I lean against him, desperate to feel his arm around my shoulder. I suppose I'm craving attention to replace the lonely feeling I'm carrying around like excess baggage and although he's probably being just kind, my needy heart is begging for more.

We reach my room, and he stops and smiles, his blue eyes twinkling in the dusky light.

"Here you go Cinderella, safe and sound. I'll wait until you get inside and make sure to lock the door behind you."

"I thought this was a safe place. Are you telling me I should be on my guard?" I giggle and he grins. "No, but it has been known for a stray guest to wander into the wrong room after a few too many cocktails, and I would hate for you to deal with that."

"Really? Has that happened?" My eyes are wide as I consider how I'd feel about that, and he nods.

"A few times. It's why it's best to take precautions."

It feels a little awkward now and so I take a deep breath and, with my key card in hand, whisper, "Thanks for tonight, I had a good time."

"Me too." He smiles so sweetly it's impossible not to be affected by his attention and reluctantly I let myself into my room and as the door closes behind me, I lean back on it and sigh. What a night.

∽

DESPITE THE AMOUNT of alcohol I consumed last night, I am awake bright and early and full of enthusiasm for once. The view certainly helps as I walk out onto the balcony and see the calm blue sea catching the early morning sun. I watch a figure jogging on the sand, and they look up and wave. Feeling a little self-conscious, I wave back and wonder if they are a guest or staff member? They are too far away to tell.

I shower and pull on the uniform provided and feel a little trepidation grow for today. I really hope I'm good at this because I'm not sure what I'll do if I'm sent back to England early.

Tying my long dark hair in a low ponytail, I apply minimum make-up and grab my key. Then, with a deep breath, I venture outside and just hope I'm good enough.

As I make the short walk to reception, I pass a couple out for an early morning stroll who nod pleasantly. "Lovely morning."

"Yes–it is." I smile as I pass and even though it's early, the sun is already warming my skin, making me feel happier than I have in some time. It doesn't take long to reach the place I'm going to work, and I'm relieved to see Diana waiting for me with a huge smile on her face.

"Morning Katrina, did you sleep well?"

"Like a log."

She grins. "I do after a party night. Thank goodness they're not every night. I couldn't cope."

"Same." I giggle as she rolls her eyes. "Drew loves to make a cocktail and corrupt the newbies. I hope it wasn't too much."

"No, everyone was very nice."

She nods her approval and says quickly, "Anyway, I'm guessing you haven't eaten yet if you came straight from your room. Why don't we grab a bite and discuss the day?"

"We can do that?"

I'm surprised because I thought we would be needed here, and she grins. "We'll just leave the bell out instead. If someone rings it, one of Chester's assistants will fill in for us. It's not busy though and most guests are probably having breakfast, anyway. It's the perfect time."

We head through the door that Chester took yesterday, and she directs me to a small building behind the main one.

"Staff canteen." She grins. "You'll spend a lot of time in here because the food is seriously good and there's lots to do in your downtime. Pool, card games, a massive tv. You name it, the resort provides it."

"They seem very good to their staff."

"They are." She grins. "I love it here. There really is no reason not to and there's absolutely nothing to worry about."

Feeling happier, I sigh with relief. "That's good to know. I'm guessing my six weeks will fly past and I'll be devastated to leave."

I don't miss the curious look in her eye as she says in a whisper, "Six weeks?"

"Yes, I'm due back to finish college after the summer break."

"I see." She looks thoughtful, and it worries me a little.

"Did you think I'd be here longer then?"

"It's fine." She smiles. "I just thought you were here to stay long term."

We head inside the canteen, and I can see what she means. This place has everything and is furnished way better than any canteen I have ever been to. White tables with cushioned chairs are dotted around the room. Several settees are also placed around low glass tables, facing a gigantic television screen.

There are a few curious glances thrown my way as we head inside and Diana says loudly, "Hey, guys. This is Katrina, Darcey's replacement."

It feels a little overwhelming as they stare at me with obvious interest and Diana says in a hushed whisper, "They'll introduce themselves, so don't worry about introductions now. Let's help ourselves to some food and grab a table by the window."

The breakfast is laid out buffet style and there appear to be items here to suit everyone's taste. I decide on some fresh fruit and a few pastries, and Diana loads her plate high with scrambled egg and bacon, grabbing some toast from the side. We help ourselves to orange juice and I follow her over to a table by the window where the sun is shining on the other side.

"I'm ravenous." She groans as she tucks into her plate of food, and I am beginning to wish I'd done the same. It all looks amazing and as I pick at my fruit, she says between mouthfuls. "Today I'll show you how reception works. It's pretty easy and you'll soon get the hang of it. We'll stagger our lunches and then once we're off the hook, we can go to the beach if you like."

"We can do that?"

I'm surprised at how accommodating this place is, and she nods. "Sure, we have the run of the place along with the guests. Chester encourages us to mix. It brings life to the place. I like to grab a bed on the sand and watch the sun go down with one of Drew's cocktails. It's also known as living your best life."

She grins and I'm beginning to understand what she means and thinking of Darcey and Jenny, I wonder why anyone would want to leave this paradise.

As we sit and chat, I notice Adam carrying a tray of food from the kitchen and whisper, "Tell me about Adam. He seemed so angry last night."

"He always is." She rolls her eyes. "Listen, honey, Adam is what's known as an angry soul. The only person he could tolerate was Jenny, and she left a few weeks ago. Since then, he's been sulking about it and generally getting on everyone's nerves."

"Were they together then?"

I'm wondering if they had an argument, or if it was because of what Nate told me, and she nods. "Yes, they were partners. He really seemed to like her, and we all thought they were the perfect match. She was the only one who could drag a smile from his face, so it's no wonder he's retreated into his shell now she's gone."

I say quickly, "Partners as in…"

"A couple, honey. You know, romantically involved."

"Poor Adam, he must feel lonely. Why did she leave?" I feel sorry for him and Diana shrugs. "Beats me. She was here one day and gone the next. Nobody even saw her go."

"Nate told me he took her to the mainland."

"Did he? Then that's where she went."

I look up and see Adam staring at me with an intense look and I shiver a little. There's something not right about him, and it seems as if he's the only one unhappy about being here. Maybe I should find out why, because as far as I can tell, he has no reason. Then I think back on his warning, and something tells me I'm about to find out whether I like it or not.

9

Diana was right, and this job is so easy I feel fully trained inside of ten minutes. It's just a case of welcoming guests when they check in and making sure they have everything they need. If they need us, we're here to help and we don't even have to take phone calls or work on a computer because everything is carefully laid out in a huge leather-bound book Diana calls the oracle. It has several entries detailing the day ahead, how many guests to expect, their preferences and when they leave. It's all written as one giant 'to do' list and it couldn't be any easier.

The first person I greet is a man who looks around his mid-forties, wearing an open-necked shirt and shorts. "Hey."

"Good morning, sir."

"Call me Eric."

"Thank you. I'm Katrina. How may I help you, Eric?"

"I wanted to check the time of our meeting. April wants to grab a massage, and we wanted to make sure we have long enough."

"Of course, I'll check for you."

As I consult the oracle, I see they are scheduled into the chat room at three pm with Chester and I smile. "Three pm, in the chat room. Would you like me to make the booking for April's massage? It doesn't appear to have been done."

"Sure, make it one thirty. We'll have an early lunch."

"Good choice. Consider it done."

I smile and feel a little disconcerted as his eyes drag the length of my body and he takes a long, considered look.

"How old are you?" His question surprises me, but I disguise it. "Eighteen, sir, um, Eric."

"What about your education, good grades?"

Now he's being weird, and I stutter, "So far."

"What do you mean?"

He leans a little closer and I feel myself shift awkwardly. "I have my final exams next year. I'm hoping to study medicine and need good grades."

"Interesting." He looks thoughtful. "So, you're academic then."

"I'm afraid so." I laugh nervously and he nods as if he approves. "Perfect."

He turns to leave, and it feels like the weirdest conversation ever, but I'm guessing these super–rich people don't talk about the same things as normal people like me. Brushing it off, I thank God I'm not like him and wonder if he should join a club or something to learn the art of small talk. What's wrong with passing comment about the weather? Asking me about my education and staring at me as if I'm a prize exhibit at a cattle market is just plain weird.

"Hey, beautiful."

I look up and see Nate leaning casually on the desk and my heart does a little happy dance inside.

"Hi."

I smile and feel a little shy around him and feel annoyed at myself. I know it's because I'm attracted to him and am preparing my heart for a brutal break.

He nods towards the beach. "Fancy that tour?"

"Sure, but I'm waiting for Diana to come back from lunch before I can go."

"Then meet me at the water sports hut on the beach. We may as well start there."

He winks as he heads off and I feel a deliciously warm feeling inside. Nate is every wish I ever had rolled up into a very desirable male and just the fact he's giving me so much attention is making me fall for him in a very big way.

Trying to distract my thoughts, I gaze down at the oracle and wonder about the chat room. What is that all about? Surely I should know, just in case anyone asks.

Studying the list, I see they are the only people meeting Chester today and I expect it's to discuss their stay here and possibly book for next year, or something along those lines. Maybe this is similar to one of those time-share talks that attracts people with a special offer and then tries to get them to buy weeks.

Glancing down the list, I see a Mr and Mrs Mackenzie are due to be taken on a tour of the island later and Nate is the staff member scheduled next to their name. There are also entries for Sven providing personal training, someone called Rosa who is responsible for manicures it seems and a private meal in the gazebo this evening for a Mr and Mrs Potterton-Smythe.

"Hey, did I miss anything?"

I look up as Diana arrives, looking a little flushed, and she fans herself with her hand. "It's hot out there today."

"Yes, thank goodness for the air conditioning in here."

The fact it's so hot outside makes me wonder if I should change before meeting Nate on the beach during my lunch hour.

She peers over my shoulder. "Did anything happen while I was gone?"

"Just a guest called Eric who wanted to check his meeting time, which reminds me, what's the chat room all about?"

"Beats me, honey." She shrugs. "Chester likes to meet and greet the guests and they head there. Mainly because he plies them with alcohol and fancy food, and they always leave looking happier than when they went in."

"So, what do you tell the guests when they ask what the meeting is about?"

"I don't need to, they never ask. I think they know already, it's probably in the welcome pack or something."

"Aren't you curious?"

I'm surprised because how does she not know what goes on in the chat room?

"Not really. I couldn't care less what they talk about. It's probably ultra-boring, anyway. You know, these people have more money than brain cells so if Chester wants to relieve them of some of it that's down to him."

"What, like a time-share?"

She laughs out loud. "If you like. Anyway, your turn for lunch, don't hurry back, it's looking quiet today."

"What will you do?"

"I've got some learning to do, it will give me the opportunity to catch up."

"What are you learning?"

"French. Chester likes his staff to improve themselves. This place is so quiet it gives us plenty of time to improve our minds. Katie's studying Japanese, kudos to her it looks so complicated. Sven is studying for a math degree, and I believe Nate is learning accounting. The list is endless and if you take my advice, you'll decide what you want to learn while you're here. Chester will expect you to apply your mind and it may as well be something that interests you."

She pulls a folder out from under the desk and spreads it out.

"Here's mine. I'm doing ok so far but I've still got a long way to go. My exams in three months so I really need to brush up on my skills."

I see it's all paperwork and a few textbooks. She has some headphones in her hand and a small iPad that she plugs them into. "Audio learning is the best way. I can stand here learning while I work. It certainly breaks the monotony of the job." She says, rolling her eyes.

It strikes me a little strange that she stands behind a desk with no guests to serve, listening to a French lesson but I suppose it could be a lot worse and she waves me off as she mouths, "Au revoir, Katrina, passe un bon déjeuner."

She winks as I head off with a small smile on my lips. I can't help but really like Diana. She makes it impossible not to.

10

I decide against changing because I'm keen to make the most of every minute of my hour and as I walk on the beach, I congratulate myself on landing what is shaping up to be my dream job. Watching me approach is the man of those dreams, and he waves as I get nearer.

"Hey Kat, glad you made it."

As I reach him, he grins. "Welcome to the beach hut. This is where we arrange the water sports for the guest. Paddle boarding, canoes, jet skis and snorkelling. There's also the speedboat you experienced first-hand that yours truly uses to take the guests out to explore. We'll do that when we've got more time."

"Great, thanks."

Nate smiles and I stare at him with open admiration and I'm guessing he's used to that because what's not to like. He must be over 6ft tall with dirty blonde hair that he wears slightly longer on top, framing astonishingly blue eyes. His body is tanned and the result of a lot of hard work at the gym, judging from his biceps. He wears his casual clothing with style and as he perches his aviators across his eyes, he offers me his hand.

"Let me help you, this sand can be treacherous."

"Are you kidding me?" I laugh as he grins, his large hand closing around mine and settling there as if it was made to.

"Come, we'll do the tour and then grab some lunch. It's lobster today and you won't want to miss that."

I think I'm in a parallel universe where everything is five stars because who gets to eat lobster—for lunch?

"So, pretty lady, this is the beach, home of yours truly. If you take the steps over there, they lead to the pool, which you know from last night. If we go the other way, there's a gazebo on the edge looking out to sea where the private meals are served. We've had the odd wedding here too, but most of our guests are a little past that unless it's for the second or third time."

"Do many return?"

"Some do, but mostly they're new."

"How do they hear of it?"

"Usually by invite. Madelaine is our saleswoman, and she does a good job."

At the mention of my saviour, I say with interest. "Does she come here much?"

"Yes, she spends one week a month here, just to check in and keep Chester happy."

"Why?"

I'm confused, and he laughs out loud. "Chester and Madelaine are partners."

"What as in…"

"Together in every way." He grins. "You'll get used to Catalina ways, Katrina. Nearly all the staff are encouraged to pair up with someone. It keeps them happy and there aren't any vacancies for single people on this island."

"But I'm single."

I stare at him in shock, and he shrugs, "You have me."

"What do you mean?"

I'm a little taken aback, and he stops and stares straight into my eyes, saying firmly, "I'm without a current partner and you need one. Problem solved."

"A current partner."

I'm reeling from this, and he nods. "Darcey was my partner, but she left, so I'm looking for the position to be filled. You need one, so here we are."

I stare at him in shock as he shrugs. "It's for the best. We team up and they leave us alone. You get to stay, so problem solved."

"So…" I blink in shock, my mind racing like a racing car off the grid.

"We partner up and I can stay. If we don't, I must leave."

He nods. "Correct."

"But…"

I'm so confused because I don't think I've understood what partner means on Catalina and it must show because he says with a small smile, "Don't worry, you're in safe hands. Just go with the flow and you'll figure it out. All it means is that we partner up in the evenings and spend our free time together."

"So, friends really." My voice is getting higher the more I digest this information, and he grins, with a slightly devilish look twinkling in his eyes.

"Maybe more. Who knows, it could be fun."

Wishing there was a fan handy to help with the surge of heat setting me on fire, I follow him as he points out several places on our walk. The trouble is, I can't even concentrate because what is this – Love Island or something? Couple up or go home. Surely Madelaine would have told me about that. Then again, I would choose Nate in a heartbeat because he is everything I like. Then I think of Adam and wonder about his own stay on the island.

"Does that mean Adam has to leave?" I blurt out my question and Nate stills for a second.

"Possibly, if he doesn't play the game."

"The game?"

Now I'm even more confused and Nate shrugs. "Adam has been told to partner with Chloe. He's refusing but Chester will talk him round."

"But that's so cold." I can't believe what I'm hearing, and he shakes his head. "Adam's a fool if he refuses. Chester's a good guy, but I wouldn't want to upset him and if Adam doesn't play ball, his time here is done."

"He may prefer that. Maybe he fell in love with Jenny and will follow her."

"He probably will if he turns his back on Chloe. He should just learn to roll with it and enjoy the perks of the job instead."

He squeezes my hand and says brightly, "Let's go and eat and I'll show you the staff area after."

We head into the cool air-conditioned canteen, and I sigh with relief at the respite from the heat outside. It's a cool oasis of delight, judging by the feast laid out before me. Beautifully prepared lobster is resting on mixed salad leaves with delicious looking salads in bowls nestling nearby. Grabbing a couple of sparkling cocktails, Nate hands them to me. "Go and grab a table, babe. I'll bring the food."

Feeling as if I'm having an out-of-body experience, I take a seat at an empty table overlooking the spa building and look around with a keener interest than before because Nate has just dropped a huge bombshell and I need to think about what it means for me. Noticing the tables are filled with couples, all male and female, I pay particular attention to them. Many are holding hands, some laughing and gazing flirtatiously into each other's eyes. I watch one man gently stroke the girl's face opposite him and it strikes me that every staff member here is around my own age or slightly older. In fact, other than Chester and the guests, it's a very young crew and I wonder about that.

Nate heads back carrying plates laden with food and says happily, "I never miss lobster. It's always good and Joseph, our head chef, is particularly gifted."

"Does he have a partner?" I am so intrigued I can't think past this strange requirement, and Nate nods. "Fran, she's one of the masseurs. Pretty girl with the patience of a saint. She needs to be with him as her partner because chefs are known to be volatile and he's no exception."

"Maybe that's where Adam gets it from."

He laughs. "Probably."

I look past Nate and see the man himself glowering at us from across the room and I feel awkward. He looks as if he hates us both and it puts me on edge.

Nate is eating his food as if he's dying from starvation and as I nibble at mine, I find I've lost my appetite, which is a shame because this food is seriously good.

Then I have an idea and say casually, "I'll grab us some water."

Nate nods and carries on eating and on shaking legs, I head toward the buffet where Adam is working, clearing away empty dishes. I'm not even sure why I thought this was a good idea and hover nervously beside the water cooler that is placed to the side, with slices of refreshing lemon infusing it. As I grab a glass, without even looking at me, Adam says in a low growl, "Meet me at the gazebo at ten tonight. Don't tell anyone."

I move away fast, my heart thumping with adrenalin and curiosity. Maybe Adam has something to tell me that I really need to know because I'm not a fool. There is something seriously weird going on here and Adam appears to be the only one who is not that happy about it. I need to know all the facts before I make up my own mind, so I decide to meet him later and find out just what this island's secret is.

11

After lunch, I head back to reception and see Diana exactly where I left her, concentrating hard and mouthing French words.

She sees me coming and pulls the headphones from her ear and smiles. "That went quickly. Did you have the lobster? It's seriously good."

My mind is so full of what I've learned and I'm not sure if I should ask but say slightly nervously, "Um, do you have a partner, Diana?"

She looks at me with interest and I see a slight grin on her face as she nods. "I see Nate told you how it works here."

"So, it's true. I thought he was spinning me a line."

"No, it's all true. We partner up and who wouldn't want that, anyway? It makes life more interesting, and you're lucky he's available. Nate is one of the good ones–enjoy."

It feels strange talking about this, and she must sense my confusion because she lowers her voice. "Listen honey. Just go with it. When I first arrived, and they threw this at me, I was much like you. It felt odd–wrong even, but Matty made me feel so welcome and secure, I was more than happy about it."

"Matty?"

"My partner. He's head of security and spends most of his days patrolling the beaches, making sure there aren't any uninvited guests. I'll introduce you later if you like."

"Thanks. It would be good to meet him."

I still have so many questions and Diana must sense that because she sighs and leans closer. "Listen, don't dwell on it. Nate's not the sort to make you do anything you're not happy with. Just enjoy his company and leave it at that. It will be boring, but if that's what you want, he won't mind."

"You mean..."

She shrugs. "Like most relationships, they progress at different speeds. Matty was an angel and gave me all the time I needed. He was seriously attentive and couldn't do enough for me, so it was inevitable I would fall for him at some point and I'm so happy I did."

"But I still don't understand. Why do we have to partner up? Surely that's not required to do the job."

Diana shrugs. "I think they do it to keep our minds on the job. Think about it. If we were all single and ready to mingle, they would have all the shit that goes with that. Arguments, cheating and jealously. It would ruin the happy vibe of the island, and that is Chester's main concern. He wants to create a couple's environment, whether it's real or not. This way the guests are happy among loved up staff members, and it keeps the mood mellow."

She sighs. "Take Adam, for instance. He's angry and is seriously bringing the atmosphere down. We are all on edge around him because he creates tension in the room. To be honest, the sooner he leaves, the better and we can carry on."

She turns away, leaving me feeling extremely concerned. This is wrong on every level. Fabricating happiness and perfection along with the interiors and the carefully swept sandy beach. Stepford in paradise springs to mind. None of its real and I can't for one moment think that's ok.

The rest of the afternoon is spent manning the desk and we only get one enquiry from a woman who wants to book a boat excursion for tomorrow. Carefully, I write down her requirements and pen Nate's name next to it. Then put a note in his cubby hole for him to collect when he's passing.

"I wonder why they don't use computers?" I look at Diana and she shrugs. "They don't need them and there's no Wi-Fi, anyway. In fact, there's not a lot of anything connecting Catalina to the outside world."

I'm stunned. "What, no communication at all?"

She laughs. "Of course there is, but it's all handled by Chester's team."

"Chester's team?"

"They work on the mainland and there are a couple of assistants in the back office. They coordinate everything and arrange connections for the guests, but not the staff."

"Don't you think that's odd?"

"I did." She pulls a face. "Now I don't care. Most of us have nothing on the mainland anyway, so who would we call?"

"What about your family?"

I'm getting more concerned as the day goes on and her face falls, making me feel bad for mentioning it.

"My family threw me out when I was eighteen."

"Why?"

I'm a little shocked at that, and she shrugs. "They told me I had to make my own way in life and their job was done. In fact, they couldn't wait to see the back of me and even ordered a cab and helped me pack."

"That's terrible."

I am seriously upset for her, and she sighs heavily. "It was a stormy relationship. Most of my teens we clashed, and I wasn't the model daughter they wanted. As soon as they could, they got rid of me."

"How do you feel about that?"

I feel bad for her, and she sighs. "I don't feel good about it, but it is what it is. There's no love lost there, and I wouldn't care if I never saw them again. Madelaine has become a second mother to me, and the island is now my home. The rest of the staff are my new family, and I'm happy with that."

"And you have Matty."

"And I have Matty." She smiles. "That's the best part of all. You know Katrina, don't overthink this place. It's really not that bad. I know it's different, but ask yourself what's bad about that? Most people would kill to live like this, and I've never known any arguments or fights, so that's got to be a good thing, surely."

I return her smile, but it will take me some time to get used to this, and then she says brightly, "Time to pack up for the day. My sunbed is calling, and Drew had better have my sundowner ready. You can join me if you like."

"Thanks." My mind is working overtime and to be honest, I just want to be alone, so I shake my head. "It's fine. I'm thinking of exploring a bit, if you don't mind."

"Sure, the offer's always there, though."

She heads off the other way and as I walk to my room, I take my troubled thoughts with me. Today has been surprising in many ways and yet I'm feeling happy about it, especially the part where I get to partner up with Nate. The trouble is, it feels as if I have no choice in the matter which has thrown me a little. An arranged coupling of the most disturbing kind and the question is, what am I going to do about it?

Once I've changed, I head out and take a different route away from the buildings. Maybe some time alone will help rearrange my confused thoughts and as I grasp the water bottle I filled from the refrigerator in my room, I set off along a track that runs around the perimeter of the resort.

Aside from a few lizards and some sweet singing birds, there is nobody else around and I'm glad about that.

I can't stop thinking of everything I've heard today and don't register where I'm walking until I hear a loud, "Excuse me!"

Peering into the distance, I see a man heading my way and my heart sinks. Now what?

He draws nearer and I see a friendly looking guy with dark hair and a slight stubble on his face. He's wearing a white polo shirt with the island logo embroidered on it and navy shorts which indicates this a member of staff I have yet to meet.

"You must be Katrina." His smile is broad, and I nod in surprise.

"Yes."

"Matty." He offers me his hand. "Diana may have told you about me."

"She did. I'm pleased to meet you, Matty."

He seems so sweet I feel comfortable with him already, and he falls into step beside me.

"So, are you exploring? Do you fancy some company?"

To be honest, I want to say no, but it would seem churlish, so I smile. "Great, um, thanks."

He waves his hand at the surroundings. "There's not a lot to see away from the resort, just sand with a bit of vegetation thrown in. I patrol several times a day just to check nobody's here that shouldn't be."

"It's small then?" It's impossible to see how big the island really is, and Matty nods. "Yes, the resort takes up most of it, but there's a nature reserve on the other side where there are some seriously rare orchids and tropical birds. You should get Nate to take you there. We have a buggy you can use. It only takes twenty minutes, and the chef will pack you a picnic."

He smiles and as his eyes twinkle, I can see why Diana fell for him so hard. Almost as if he can read minds, he whispers, "I took Diana there on a date and by the end of it she agreed to partner up with me. It's a magical place."

He winks and I feel myself blush as he says, "Nate's a great guy. He'll make a good partner for you."

"Do I have a choice?" I'm starting to feel a little railroaded and he must sense that because he stops and looks concerned. "Listen, Katrina. This island can be paradise or hell. Embrace all it has to offer, no matter how weird, and you will fall in love with it. If you fight against it, it's not so pleasant. I've been here for six months already, and I've seen many people struggle with it. Those who make it their own are happy, those who don't..." He shakes his head. "Well, they leave."

"But I'm going in six weeks, anyway. I have college and exams to sit."

I'm not sure if it's my imagination playing tricks on me, but Matty is looking at me as if I'm deranged.

"Of course." He grins. "Then enjoy it while you can; that's my advice."

He looks at his watch and says ruefully. "We should go."

"We?"

"Yes, tonight there's a general meeting and Chester will be angry if we're late. Word of advice, Katrina, don't upset Chester. That's the one rule you break at your peril."

Needing no further persuasion, I follow him, and as we head back the way I came, I just hope this meeting will answer a few questions that are now screaming for answers.

12

The meeting is being held in the canteen and, as usual, the most amazing food is laid out as snacks, along with hot drinks and a few non-alcoholic cocktails. I'm surprised at how many staff are here. Most of them I have never seen, along with many I have. I feel the curiosity in the room as they watch me with interest and so I'm glad when a low voice whispers, "Hey, babe, there you are. Come and sit with me."

Nate slips his hand in mine and guides me towards a table

where Katie and Sven are sitting, chatting. They smile when we join them and Katie says warmly, "How was your day?"

"Good, thanks." She leans in. "You know I'm always here if you have any questions about, um, anything really."

She laughs as Sven drops his arm around her shoulders and kisses her cheek softly and it makes me wonder if this is really so bad. I mean, if it makes you feel this good, maybe it's something I should explore rather than turn my back on. It could be an experience that could be the making of me.

Nate leans in, "I hope I didn't scare you off earlier. Maybe we should spend the evening together and get to know one another as friends first."

"Thanks." I feel a little relieved. "I'd like that."

He smiles and I don't think I've ever met such a gorgeous guy. He is easily one of the best-looking men here and I should be flattered that he is paying me so much attention. Looking around the room, I see much the same at every table. Young couples either gazing into each other's eyes or chatting with the next couple. I notice Adam sitting beside Chloe, who is gazing at him as if he hung the moon. He appears to be listening to something the guy opposite him is saying and now he has ditched his angry frown. I can see how attractive he is. In fact, this whole room is like something out of Stepford, and I wonder if that was the inspiration for Chester's utopia.

Then the man himself heads into the room and cuts a commanding figure in his white chinos and navy polo shirt. Like every other man here, he is groomed to perfection and always appears freshly showered with nothing out of place. It's impossible not to admire men like these and as he scans the room, his gaze falls on me and he smiles when he sees Nate's arm casually slung along the back of my chair.

For some reason, I crave his approval, which shows me how this place is already messing with my mind. The last thing I want is to give him any reason to ask me to leave so I should try hard to fit in. Despite how strange Catalina Island is, it is also paradise and for a girl with nothing, that is a very strong reason to stay.

"Quiet everybody and I'll begin so you can head off for the evening."

The room falls silent and watch as he sits casually on one of the tables and smiles. "I just wanted to extend a warm welcome to Katrina Darlington, who joined us yesterday."

I sink a little further in my seat as the entire room turns to look at me. Nate strokes the back of my neck in a show of support, and it certainly doesn't feel unpleasant.

Chester carries on. "Make her welcome and show her how things work around here." He smiles at me. "I'm always happy to answer any questions myself and you are welcome to seek me out anytime, day or night."

I smile nervously as he goes on to say, "Anyway, as you all know, Katrina is Darcey's replacement who left us a couple of weeks ago. She had an offer of work from one of our guests and just couldn't say no. I'm sure you will join me in wishing her well for her future and hope she comes back to visit one day."

The room murmurs and claps and I wonder what this job is she apparently couldn't turn down.

He seems to look directly at Adam as he says in a more serious tone. "Jenny Grady also left through personal choice, leaving Adam without a partner."

My heart jumps as the focus of the room falls on the angry chef and I'm surprised to see a smile on his face as he lifts the hand of the girl beside him and Chester laughs. "However, Chloe has stepped into Jenny's shoes and agreed to partner him, so I'm sure you will all join me in congratulating them on their decision."

The room erupts with applause, and I join in, feeling slightly confused. Adam is smiling and looking extremely happy about things as he lifts Chloe's hand to his lips and makes a big show of kissing it as she blushes beside him.

Gone is the angry frown and sullen expression and in its place is one of happiness and joy, which changes him completely. His face has relaxed and his eyes twinkle making him more approachable. His light brown hair hangs slightly longer than most, framing gorgeous green eyes. Like most of the guys here, he has an amazing suntan making him look healthy, and he obviously works out because there's nothing but muscle on his body. It appears that health and happiness are the result of living on Catalina, and I'm surprised at the disappointment I feel when I look at the guy who growled with determination a few hours earlier asking me to meet him at the gazebo later. It makes me wonder if that's still on and now I feel even more confused than ever.

Chester holds up his hand and the room falls silent. "We have a couple of guests leaving tomorrow. Mr and Mrs Barker-Smythe. Nate will have the pleasure of escorting them to the mainland and I would like you to make a point of finding them and wishing them safe travel. We have a new couple replacing them, Mr and Mrs De Vere, who I'm told are difficult to please. Pull out all the stops on this one because we don't want any failures on Catalina and I'm sure I don't need to remind you it's important they get the full experience."

He looks at his watch and says pleasantly, "That wraps things up here except ...."

A huge smile breaks out across his face, and he says happily, "Madelaine will be arriving tomorrow for one week, so make a point of arranging a one to one with her. Obviously, the main reason she's here is rest and recuperation, but she will be keen to catch up with every one of you."

He looks across the room and his eyes fall on our table as he says with a smile. "Nate, don't make any plans for dinner tomorrow night. You will dine with us. Bring Katrina, the usual place."

Nate nods and for some reason, I feel quite excited at the prospect of spending time with Madelaine. I have so many questions to ask her and am keen to discover how she knows my parents and how she knew they had died. It's been bugging me because I can't think who told her. Was it Mr Frobisher, or did she read it somewhere? I am struggling to remember events afterwards and wonder if there's some kind of obituary list posted somewhere.

Chester says in a loud voice, "Ok, you're off the hook. Go and make the most of the rest of the sunshine and enjoy your evening. There's no need to mix tonight because the guests have an evening's entertainment lined up and only Drew and Imogen are required to serve drinks and tidy up after them.

I look across and see Drew with his arm around a girl who is obviously more than happy about that, and I sigh inside. Aside from Adam, I haven't seen a frown on anyone's face and even he appears to have changed his mind as I watch Chloe gaze at him with adoration as he clasps her hand in his and stares lovingly into her eyes. I'm not sure why I feel disappointed about that, but I have no time to dwell on it as Nate whispers, "Come on, I'll carry on with our tour of the island."

The staff are all dispersing and as we leave, Sven says quickly, "Are you still up for training later, Nate?"

"Sure, wouldn't miss it."

"Good. I'll meet you in the gym, usual time."

"See you then."

Nate slings his arm around my shoulder and pulls me along with him, and I can't say I'm unhappy about that. As we head outside away from the noise, he says with concern, "I work out with Sven three times a week and his time is limited. I'm sorry, but I'll have to leave you at 9.30. Maybe you should get an early night or look Katie up for company."

"It's fine. I'm quite tired. I'll just chill out on my own."

I'm quick to make excuses because this is good news. At least I can slip off and meet Adam, always supposing he's there. I'm kind of hoping he is because I'm burning with curiosity to discover the secrets of Catalina and out of anybody here, I think he is the one to tell me.

13

Nate is good company. In fact, I don't think I've ever felt so comfortable around anyone this quickly. Then again, nobody has ever paid me so many compliments or given me their undivided attention like this, and it's a powerful weapon. The more time I spend here—with him, the harder I fall and when his hand slips into mine, I am just happy it's there.

We stroll around the grounds and Nate points out the various bungalows, much like Chester did, and tells me about the guests and their lives. He reminisces about ones with a funny story to tell of their stay here. One couple fell asleep on the sunbeds one afternoon with their glasses on and wore the evidence of that for the rest of their stay. Another couple had a massive argument by the pool and the wife pushed the man in and told him she was leaving and never coming back. They were found a few hours later making passionate love in Nate's boathouse and then again the next day in the spa, where they were having a couple's massage. One couple were known for trying to swap partners with just about anyone who was up for that and the more he makes me laugh, I fall a little deeper under his spell.

He leads me to the gazebo on the small headland that juts out to sea, and I feel a shiver of anticipation when I think about meeting Adam here under the veil of darkness later.

However, now as we watch the sun setting in the sky, I allow myself one moment of indulgence as Nate's hand clasps mine and he pulls me gently against his side. Everything is magical on Catalina and as the slight breeze calms my heated skin, I watch nature delivering the most spectacular show. "It's so beautiful." I gasp with delight as the sun hovers on the horizon and Nate says in a husky voice, "You are beautiful, Kat. I just want you to know that."

I half turn and steal a look and feel the blush staining my cheeks as a surge of longing shoots through me. This is too much, an assault on my feelings, and as he steps closer, his lips hover dangerously close to mine. He reaches up and gently smooths away the strand of hair that dances around my eyes and, as his hands cup my face on either side, he lowers his lips to mine with no invitation. As they brush against my own, I part mine willingly and as he kisses me slowly and leisurely, I allow every delicious minute of it. In fact, I could kiss him all day because he is so sweet, protective even, and it feels so good.

As kisses go, this is the best I've ever had and as he deepens the kiss, I feel a surge of longing spark into life. I want this. I want him and I can't fight it anymore. Catalina Island has woven its spell around my heart and I'm giving in as the last remaining ounce of fight drains from me because of *this* kiss.

He kisses me as if I'm the most precious thing in his life and it wraps me in desire and the promise of a bright future with him. Here on Catalina Island, where only the invited get to enjoy its pleasure, all the doubts in my mind are erased as I jump headfirst into something I want more than anything.

He pulls back and smiles, saying softly, "I won't apologise for kissing you, Katrina because I've wanted to do that for some time now."

"It's fine." My voice quivers a little, and I stare at him with a small smile on my lips.

He leans in again and this time pulls me harder against him and this kiss is different. It's more of a promise as he lights a trail of desire inside that is fast running away with me. I want him. I want Nate because I would be mad not to. The setting is the most romantic one I have ever experienced, and he is the best-looking guy I have ever met who is focusing all his attention on me.

The kiss lasts the entire time it takes for the sun to retreat behind the horizon and when he pulls back, Nate smiles, his eyes sparkling in the dusky light. "Thank you."

"For what?" I feel a little self-conscious now and he whispers, "For making me the happiest man on Catalina right now."

I can't even answer him because I am way out of my depth on this and he says huskily, "We are going to have so much fun together. This island is the most romantic place on earth and if you allow it, it can be everything you ever wanted in life."

It would be so easy to think dreams can come true. That Catalina Island is the only place I need in life. Out here, standing on the edge of paradise with the most handsome man I have ever met paying me compliments, I could be excused anything. I want this, I want him, and any doubts surfacing are brushed angrily away. Maybe it's time to be selfish and accept everything they are offering me because what can be that bad about it, anyway?

It feels good touring the island with a loving companion. Nate holds my hand, and we frequently stop to share a leisurely kiss that becomes more intense as the time slips by. Soon we are making out behind trees, against walls and even standing out in the open and I don't recognise the person he has unleashed. This isn't me. I'm not *that* girl. I'm the one everyone passes by for a brighter, shinier one. But here on this private island, I am a queen and Nate is my king.

∽

WE HEAD to the canteen for dinner, and I'm surprised to see it's been transformed tonight. Candles flicker on every table with beautiful flowers arranged in cut glass vases, creating a romantic atmosphere. "What's happening?" I stare around in awe, and Nate grins. "Couple's night. I should have warned you."

"It looks impressive."

He nods and holding my hand, guides me over to the buffet where I stare in awe at the array of dishes waiting to tempt us. There is every kind of fish going, along with soups, salad and all kinds of meat. Nate hands me a small spoon laden with caviar and pops it into my mouth, feeding me like a baby. As the slightly intense taste overpowers my taste buds, he stares into my eyes and says in a whisper, "The food of love, Katrina. How does it taste?"

I smile. "Astonishing."

He lifts an oyster shell from the table and says in a low voice,

"Allow me." I'm surprised when he holds it to my lips and pulls my head slightly back, and as my lips part, he slides the delicacy down my throat. "What about that?"

I swallow and shiver. "Not so good."

He laughs, picking up a sparkling glass of champagne and holds it to my lips. "I find it's best washed down with the finest champagne."

If I feel self-conscious standing in full view of everyone with Nate feeding me seafood, you wouldn't know it because I am more than happy about this. It's so powerful. The man, the setting and the surroundings. Who wouldn't fall in love with this and any inhibitions or doubts I had are becoming a distant memory? I deserve this attention. It's *my* time and after the pain of the past few weeks, this is my reward. So, I am going to seize this opportunity and worry about the repercussions some other time because Catalina Island has woven its spell around my heart, and I am happy to go along for the ride.

14

Nate heads to the gym with the promise of meeting me for breakfast in the morning. As first dates go, this one was sweeter than most and he leaves me with a lingering kiss fresh on my lips and a smile of contentment on my face. It feels so good to wrap myself in magic for a moment because there hasn't been a lot to smile about lately. It still catches me when I least expect it. A memory that sparks the sudden realisation I will never see my parents again. The anguish of loss and the pain of betrayal when I remember they signed my future away in a cold, hard contract.

Maybe a fling with Nate is just what I need to help me forget. A selfish indulgence before I return to harsh reality and a few months of hard study. My future is looking uncertain now and I need this time to clear my head and decide on my future. However, all of that can wait because Catalina Island has given me a safety net to fall into and I should make the most of everything it has to offer before I leave forever.

I wait until I'm sure the coast is clear and quickly dress in black leggings and a black t-shirt, so I don't stand out in the darkness. It feels wrong on every level to be doing this at all. A clandestine meeting of the strangest kind and my cover story, should I need one, is that I couldn't sleep with all the excitement and decided to head out for a moonlit run.

Tying my long brown hair behind me in a scrunchie, I pull on my trainers and slip outside the door. The only sound I hear is of the crickets chattering in the nearby bushes, providing a concerto of the most natural kind.

I gently jog along the path and take a sharp left, away from the path that leads down to the beach. It strikes me how silent it is on this private island. Only the sounds of nature serenade me as I move stealthily along the path, my senses on high alert while waiting to be discovered at any moment.

My own breathing is ragged, and I struggle to keep my cool because the anxiety is riding high within me and I'm fearing being caught, which surprises me because surely, I'm doing nothing wrong, although it certainly feels that way.

I see the Gazebo like a giant shadow looming in the distance and my heart quickens as I draw near, wondering if Adam will even be there.

As I slow my pace, I listen keenly for any sign of human company, but only hear the waves crashing against the shoreline. I venture silently towards the edge, which stares across the ocean, appearing to stretch into infinity.

As I wait, I feel my heart thumping and then I hear a soft, "Katrina."

Peering into the darkness, it appears to be coming from the edge of the rock face and I slowly inch towards it and whisper, "Yes."

Then I hear a gruff, "Sit on the edge and jump down. There's a ledge beneath and I'll catch your hand so you don't fall."

I can't see a thing and really don't want to do this, but curiosity has grabbed my common sense and is holding it to ransom, so I do as he says and dangle my legs over the edge of the rock face.

A hand catches my ankle, making me jump, and a low voice whispers, "Lower yourself down and I'll guide your foot onto the ledge."

This feels so wrong and yet the excitement causes an adrenalin rush I don't want to lose and as I do as he says, I soon find myself standing on a large ledge out of sight.

I can just about make out Adam in the darkness and he says urgently, "Come, there's a small cave in here where we can talk."

This feels so alien to me, yet my spirit of adventure is taking over, and I inch along the ledge next to him, conscious of the waves crashing below us.

He pulls me into a hole in the side of the cliff edge and I note a flickering candle standing in a jar on the floor. It illuminates the cave and I look around in surprise. There are no luxuries here, just the damp spray from the sea and a few lingering pieces of seaweed that don't make for a pleasant smell. In fact, this place is seriously creepy and yet I don't feel afraid, just curious, and Adam whispers, "Sorry about the venue but it's all we've got. Take a seat. It's not that comfortable, but it's better than standing."

I crouch down and sit with my legs underneath me for added support, and Adam sits opposite and reaches for a flask.

"Here, I made us some coffee to help take the chill off."

I'm so grateful for something to distract me from how I'm feeling right now. Nervous, excited, afraid, and curious, all mixed up in a lethal cocktail of foolishness.

"I'm sorry, Katrina." Adam sighs. "You must be wondering what the hell is going on."

"A little."

He laughs. "Just a little, then you're brighter than I first gave you credit for."

He grins. "Anyway, I just wanted to reach out to you before Nate did irreversible damage."

"What do you mean?" I'm not liking the sound of this, and he looks worried.

"Don't trust him. In fact, trust no one but especially not Nate."

"Why not?" Now I'm feeling decidedly uncomfortable, and he looks angry.

"Nate is tight with Chester and Madelaine. There are no secrets between them, and they run this place as a family."

"You mean they're related?"

He nods. "Nate's Chester's son."

"I don't understand. He told me something else entirely." I'm confused and Adam growls, "They weren't his real parents."

My mind is scrambled, and I say quickly, "I'm sorry Adam, you'll have to explain. None of this makes any sense."

Adam shakes his head and looks a little sad, which surprises me. "Nate is Chester's biological son. His parents, Mr, and Mrs Miller, are just his adoptive ones, although their names will be on his birth certificate."

"How do you know?"

This is a strange conversation, and Adam lowers his voice.

"Listen, I've been here a while and discovered a few secrets of this place that would blow your mind and I'm pretty sure you feel it too. Don't you agree there's an undercurrent of something sinister here? I mean…" He exhales sharply. "This place is perfect on the outside for a very good reason. If you scratch the surface, though, it's a different canvas underneath. You may wonder how I know; well do you remember Jenny?"

"The girl who asked to leave."

"Yes. She was my partner, and I never suspected a thing. Like you, I was encouraged to pair up with someone and I liked her. I genuinely did. She liked me too, and we were happy. Then I felt her withdrawing from me. She looked worried and her eyes held shadows that weren't there before."

"Did she tell you why?"

"Not at first, but I kept on asking and one night she broke down and told me something I still can't believe now."

"What?" I'm mesmerised by this and can't even breathe until I hear this secret and he says in a low voice, "She said her friend Darcey told her a secret that she must never tell a living soul and she was struggling with what that may mean for her."

"Did she tell you what it was?"

"Yes." He sighs heavily and leans back against the cave wall.

"Darcey was with Nate at the time, you know, partnered up with him and apparently happy. Then Chester started paying her attention. At first, she thought it was because of Nate. They were close, but at the time she didn't realise how close. Anyway, he started flirting with her, which made her feel special. I suppose he turned her head, and they started an affair."

"With his own son's girlfriend." I'm shocked and Adam laughs bitterly. "At least that's what she thought. Jenny told me Darcey had decided Chester was a better option and had designs on Madelaine's place, both in his bed and taking her job. She started making demands and confided in Jenny. Then one day, Darcey came to find her in tears and told her she was pregnant with Chester's baby."

"How did she know it was his? Wasn't she with Nate at the time?"

"Apparently they didn't have that kind of relationship and Chester didn't believe in condoms."

"That's disgusting." I feel physically sick as I think about this sordid act of betrayal on every level, and Adam nods. "Inevitably, Darcey fell pregnant with Chester's baby. She thought it would earn his support and a place by his side. Madelaine, however, wasn't too happy about that."

"She knew?" I stare at him incredulously and he nods.

"Darcey said she gave her an ultimatum. Leave Catalina and have her baby on the mainland with the support of a couple who were desperate for a child. Walk away at the end without the child and they would set her up in luxury and she would never have to work again. If she wanted to return to Nate on Catalina, she had that choice, but Chester was no longer interested."

"So, she's having the baby and Chester is ok about all this. I mean, it's his baby too?"

He nods. "Jenny told me Darcey was keen to have the baby and leave it with its new parents and return to Catalina. She wanted Chester, not money, and Jenny was afraid for her. Chester wasn't bothered about the kid and thought this was the best solution all round. Jenny wanted her to tell someone, get help, but Darcey just laughed and said Madelaine's days were numbered and she was going to go ahead and have the baby and return to claim her man."

"Do you think she will?"

"I expect she'll try, but Madelaine will probably block that from happening."

"So why was Jenny afraid?"

"Because when Darcey left, Chester focused his attention on her."

"You mean…" He nods, looking so disgusted I understand where it's coming from now.

"He started paying Jenny attention. When I was working, he sought her out and started flattering her with attention. He told her there were lots of perks in being his 'go to' girl and if she was up for it, he could make it happen."

"What a pig." I am angry on their behalf and Adam growls, "Jenny freaked out about the whole situation. Having seen what happened to Darcey, she wasn't keen on following her, so she told me one night she was leaving. She'd had enough and wanted to go back to the mainland."

"I don't blame her."

"Neither did I, and I decided to go with her. I could find a job in any restaurant, and we could start again somewhere new. Maybe rent a small apartment and save some money."

"So, what happened?"

"I woke up one day, and she was gone."

"Without telling you."

He nods, exhaling sharply. "I asked Chester where she was, and he told me Jenny had left that morning. She'd decided this wasn't the life for her anymore and rather than force her to stay, he asked Nate to drop her off at the mainland."

"Then she's safe. Maybe you could go and find her."

"I doubt that you see…"

Suddenly, a flashlight illuminates the cave and I jump in fright as a deep voice says, "What have we got here?"

15

I feel like a deer caught in headlights and I'm shocked when a low laugh accompanies the person inside the cave as Adam says, "Idiot."

As he turns off the flashlight, I'm surprised to see Matty looking at me with interest as he says in a low voice, "Where are we?"

"I was about to tell her what happened to Jenny before you crashed the party."

Matty shrugs. "Sorry, I had to wait until Chester turned in for the night and locked up the office. So, Jenny..."

Adam jerks his head towards our visitor. "It's ok, Matty is on our side."

"Our side?" Confusion is now my middle name, and they grin.

"There are a few of us." Matty says softly. "Staff members who feel uncomfortable about what's going on here. Most of us hide it well, but Adam failed the audition, and his acting skills leave a lot to be desired sometimes."

He pushes him playfully and I say with disbelief, "So does Diana..."

Matty shakes his head. "Clueless."

"Then who?"

A look passes between them, and they obviously decide to trust me a little as Adam says, "Chloe's in. It's why we partnered up, but I didn't want Chester to think it all went too easy."

"But why do you trust me? I could tell Nate and Chester and your cover would be blown?" Not that I would but I'm surprised they lowered their guard.

Matty sighs. "We wanted you in before we lost you forever. We need you, Katrina. You can help us more than you realise."

"Why would I help? For what reason?"

Another look passes between them, and Adam says roughly, "Tell her about Jenny."

Matty looks worried and Adam nods his encouragement.

"I saw Nate and Jenny leave. I was on the other side of the island, smoking in the dunes. I had my binoculars with me as usual so I can identify unwelcome visitors and I saw Jenny shouting at Nate. I was surprised because Jenny just wasn't the type to shout and then I saw him strike her across the face, causing her to fall inside the boat."

He shakes his head as Adam growls low in his throat. "Tell her the rest."

Matty looks worried but says, "I watched them through the binoculars and Nate headed out to open sea. There's no land for miles out there and certainly not close enough for the fuel he had capacity for. I didn't see Jenny stand up, and soon they were out of sight. I just knew there was something wrong and so I waited. It must have been one hour later that I saw the boat on the horizon, and it appeared that Nate was alone. I quickly jumped up and headed back to the beach, intending to meet the boat as it landed."

Adam looks down and my heart thumps with dreaded anticipation as he growls, "I called out to ask Nate if he needed a hand and he waved me away and told me he'd be fine and not to worry. I pretended not to hear him and waded in to grab the line and saw Nate kick something under the centre console. I hauled the boat in and watched him carefully, noticing a mark on his shorts that looked a lot like blood. He tried to get me to leave, and I made polite conversation to keep him there so I could stay to see what happened. I told him I saw him leave with Jenny, which is when he told me he'd dropped her off at Turtle Island."

"Where's that?"

I can't believe what I'm hearing, and he shrugs. "I've never heard of it, and it could be anywhere. Maybe she did go there and is currently enjoying life away from here, but I doubt it."

"Why?"

"Because she was wearing a bikini when she left, and all her stuff is still here. Also, when I arrived, Chester told me there was nothing but ocean in that direction and a reef that was inhabited by sharks. He even joked that it would be a good place to dispose of unwanted guests because nobody would ever find their bodies."

"Oh my god, you don't think…"

Adam hisses. "Matty left Nate to it and hid behind the beach hut. He watched Nate retrieve a knife from under the console and it was covered in something that looked a lot like blood. Nate tossed it into the ocean and when he left the boat, reached down and wiped the blade on the sand before putting it in a box used for baiting fish."

"Do you think he could have used it for that reason?"

Adam says angrily, "Of course he did, but the bait was a lot larger than normal and a good meal for many hungry sharks."

I actually feel sick and a little dizzy as they insinuate that the man I just kissed stupid is a cold-blooded killer.

Adam says in a gentler voice, "We don't know for sure, but we wanted to warn you. Strange things go on here and we need to act."

"What can we do?" I'm still not sure and Matty whispers, "We have a tentative plan, but that's all it is. We need to make sure its watertight because if we do this, their operation must be destroyed forever. We just wanted to sign you up and hope you'll help."

I fall silent as I digest this information and I can tell they are nervous due to the sudden tense atmosphere that lingers in the air.

My voice shakes as I whisper, "I'll try. What do you want me to do?"

Matty says, "We're not sure yet, but don't let on you know to Nate. Keep guarded around him and don't fall for his charms like every girl before you. Just be patient and look at everything with a questioning mind, knowing we are trying to work things out ."

Matty looks at his watch. "I should go. Diana will be looking for me. I said I'd only be twenty minutes while I checked the beach."

He jumps up with a reassuring smile. "Thanks, Katrina, but

don't worry. You're new here and they won't target you for a while, at least."

"Target me. What do you mean?"

Adam growls, "Chester evidently likes what his son has. Keep your distance from him and know he's just spinning you a story. Enjoy time with Nate, but don't drop your guard. And don't acknowledge us in the resort. It's important nobody suspects a thing."

Matty nods. "Good advice. So, we'll meet here again on Thursday when Nate has another session with Sven, and we'll have a job for you then. Between us, we can figure out what's going on here and make our plans once we have the information."

He heads off and Adam says quickly, "We'll give him five minutes and then I'll guide you back to the Gazebo. Good idea about running. It's the perfect cover story."

We wait a few minutes and I have so many questions but know they will have to wait. Adam looks concerned and whispers, "We'll look out for you, Katrina. Don't feel as if you're alone."

"It feels that way." The tears sting behind my eyes as it all comes flooding back and, to my surprise, Adam reaches out and pulls me towards him and just feeling his arms close around me, makes me fall apart. He is so kind and just rocks me gently, holding me and rubbing comforting circles on my back and after a while, pulls back and wipes my tears away in a small act of kindness.

"It's ok, I know how it feels to be alone."

"You do?"

I sniff and don't miss the sad look in his eyes, even in the darkness. "We're all alone." His voice is soft, outlined in sadness. "Ask anyone their story and they've either lost their parents or been disowned by them. That alone should ring the alarm bells and I'm guessing if we all shared our stories, they're not that different."

"That's strange in itself."

"Yes, it appears to be a common trend, telling me it's no coincidence."

"In what way?"

"Think about it. Who better to work here than people with no life outside of Catalina? Young adults who don't have the courage or knowledge to make it on their own. Desperate people with nowhere else to go and nobody to miss them or question where they are. It's an obvious pattern and makes me guarded. Take Jenny, for instance. She was an only child, like every other person here. Her parents died, and she had nowhere else to go. Sound familiar?"

An icy feeling chills me inside. "Are we safe?"

He shakes his head. "All the time we play by the rules. You see, Katrina, it's why this place appears so perfect. It's run by fear. Those who question it are biding their time, searching for answers and doing what they must to survive. The only way out of here is in Nate's boat, and only if they allow it. Many people have left this island, usually under sudden circumstances. When somebody new comes, its vital they fit in, and they pull out all the stops. Luxurious accommodation, amazing food and a partner who makes you feel loved and settled. All of this is designed to disguise the harsh reality of everyone's future here, and it's up to us to fight for survival."

"What do I have to do?" My voice shakes as I wait for instruction and he whispers, "You will be in the perfect position to find out information. Your dinner with his family tomorrow is important. Madelaine isn't here often and now you know about this, you can look for anything that could help us. Being in reception gives you an added advantage and you can see an overview of what's happening daily. The most important thing we need is information, and that's difficult to obtain. It's why they write everything in that book and allow no internet. We need to listen and absorb and work out a plan which may take more time than we have."

"Are we in danger, then?"

My heart thumps as Adam nods, his eyes flashing with anger. "If they suspect, then yes, so you must draw on your acting skills and play the game. Matty has uncovered a lot and has a certain level of access, but all the secrets we need are locked away in Chester's office. Nobody has the key, which makes it difficult to find anything out. Just keep your eyes and ears open and report back when we meet. We'll find a way out of this madness if we work together."

His smile is the reassurance I need and he says with a sigh, "It's time to go. If you need to talk, I'm around; just don't get caught asking."

He leads me back onto the ledge and as the spray from the sea hits me, I don't even register it. My mind is a turbulent sea of its own and I'm definitely not going to sleep tonight as I process everything I've heard. I jog back to my room and don't even remember the journey and as I turn in for the night, I hope to God I wake up tomorrow and this has all been a very bad dream.

16

The morning delivers a fresh burst of sunshine that burns away the drama of the night before. As I wake to a beautiful day in paradise, I almost believe I dreamt what happened last night.

After showering and changing into a freshly laundered uniform, I prepare for the day ahead and the gentle tap on the door reminds me I'm having breakfast with Nate.

My heart bangs with nerves as I open the door and see him leaning on the wall outside, looking like every fantasy I ever had.

He's certainly good looking and everything I could want in a man, except for one thing – he's a murderer, apparently.

You would hardly know it though because his open, honest face smiles with interest and he reaches out and pulls me close to his freshly showered body that smells so intoxicating.

"Hey, I missed you last night."

I laugh, the nerves fluttering inside me like a trapped moth to a flame. "No you didn't."

He bends down and whispers, "I did, and I know it's early days, but I'm falling fast for you pretty lady. You have captured me in your web."

He tilts my face to his and kisses me in a leisurely fashion, and I hate the fact I love every second of his attention. Maybe Adam and Matty are wrong, and there was a perfectly good explanation for Jenny's disappearance. They surely don't have all the facts and tales of kidnapping and murder seem so fanciful in the cold light of day.

As we walk to the canteen, he maintains polite conversation, which I'm glad about after the deep one last night. "Did you sleep well?"

"Fine, although I think the jog helped."

"You went jogging?"

I've decided to set in place my cover story to explain my night-time activity just in case anyone sees me. "Yes, it helps clear my mind and relax. I went jogging last night, and it felt good to have some time alone. It's been quite intense since I arrived, and I still have emotions to deal with."

"Your parents?" He sounds concerned and the tears prick behind my eyes as I think about the two people I miss like crazy. "It's easy to forget when you're away from things that trigger the memories, but when I'm alone, they come back to hurt me."

He squeezes my hand. "Then I won't leave you alone."

"What do you mean?" Now I'm worried that I've talked

myself into a situation I'm not going to like, and he stops suddenly and smiles into my eyes. "Maybe you should move in with me and let me chase those moments away. You don't have to be on your own; I could help you through your grief."

I really feel like kicking myself right now because how stupid can one woman be? Backtracking fast, I laugh self-consciously. "No, um, it's fine. I'm just being stupid. To be honest, I need to be on my own to deal with this. I don't know what I was thinking."

He looks so concerned it makes my heart weep bitter tears of 'just my luck.' The first time a man shows me any attention, the first time a man like Nate shows me interest, he turns out to be a psychopathic murderer with a crazy family. It almost makes me laugh hysterically, and I try desperately to pull myself together and breathe in a big dose of reality. Adam and Matty must be wrong about Jenny, and that is what I need to focus on to get through this day. I can't believe their story for my own sanity, so I smile and lighten my voice a little. "Thanks for the offer. I'm just being an idiot. So, how was your work out with Sven?"

"Good thanks. I must say I look forward to them. He can only spare three hours a week, though, and I wish it was longer. Left to my own devices, I don't work nearly as hard, and I need him to push me to extremes."

"Does he work with the other staff?"

"Yes, we all get one-on-one time with him as well as the guests. He's a great guy and never complains. So disciplined too, a good addition to our family."

"Has he been here long?" I'm curious to know, and he shakes his head. "Less than a year."

"Who has been here the longest?"

He takes a minute to answer. "Joseph, I suppose."

He looks a little guarded, which raises my own defences, and he frowns. "Other than Joseph, who has been here as long as Chester, I think it would be me."

"How long ago was that?"

"Two years. When I turned eighteen."

"Where did you live before?"

I'm fishing and yet it's a natural line of questioning and he stops and pulls me toward him. "My mother dropped a bombshell on me one day and I left home almost immediately."

"What did she say?"

I'm taken aback by the sudden pain in his eyes, and he says gruffly, "I was told I was adopted, and they weren't my real parents."

"That's terrible." I feel sorry for him because this is probably the truth, and he looks a little broken right now and I know a lot about how that feels, so I lean in and plant an impulsive kiss on his cheek. "I'm sorry, Nate. That must have hurt. Do you want to talk about it?"

"I'd like that, Kat. Maybe later, though. We need to eat and start work. How about meeting me for lunch? I'll arrange a picnic and we can talk then."

"Sounds like a plan."

I smile but feel my heart weeping inside. He looks how I feel, lost and desolate and despite everything I've heard, I want to help him if I can. Maybe it will bring some clarity on what's going on here and perhaps Nate is just as lost as the rest of us and needs help, too.

~

AFTER BREAKFAST I head to reception and Diana is already there.

"Hey, Katrina, did you have a good evening?"

"The best, thanks."

She grins with a knowing look in her eye. "I bet you did. I'm guessing Nate has a lot to do with that smile on your face."

I giggle self-consciously and she laughs out loud. "We are living the dream on Catalina, don't you agree?"

I nod. "It appears that we are."

She heaves open the huge leather-bound book and runs her finger down the page. "We have some guests checking out and some checking in. We should make sure everything is in place."

"How?" She taps her fingers on the desk. "Arrange for the maid to prepare the room. Make sure Nate is on hand to help with their bags and take them to the mainland. Welcome cocktails and cold towels for the guests and we always arrange a goody bag for the departing guests to take to the airport with them. Bottled water, refreshing wipes and a few snacks to keep them going."

She looks thoughtful. "If you head to the kitchen, you can arrange the welcome platter of fruit and I'll stay here. You should also look for Drew and tell him we need two cocktails for our arriving guests. I usually time it three hours from when Nate leaves. He deposits one set of guests to the taxi on the mainland and then hangs around for the new arrivals."

"Three hours. what does he do while he waits?"

"Maybe you should ask him. If it were me, I'd do a bit of shopping and maybe grab some lunch. He's lucky to get that opportunity."

"What about the staff? Do we get time on the mainland?"

She shakes her head. "No, not unless Chester agrees. I mean, we have everything we need here and if you need supplies, you add them to the delivery. There's no real need to leave, but if you feel like it, Chester allows us half a day."

My ears prick up until she laughs. "Not that it ever happens, of course."

"What do you mean?"

She shrugs. "I tried to arrange an afternoon off once and at the last minute I was as sick as a dog. The thought of travelling anywhere lost its appeal, and I decided against it."

"So, you have never left the island."

I'm surprised and she shakes her head with an accompanying deep sigh. "No, to be honest, none of us can be bothered. There's nothing on the mainland anyway and Chester and Nate pick up anything we need if we ask them."

She grins and I can tell the subject is closed as she says briskly, "Anyway, we should start work. Go and arrange the stuff with Joseph and don't be put off by his scratchy behaviour. The mans a culinary genius and we indulge his eccentricities."

I leave her to it, glad of a chance to explore a little and as I pass a few of the guests heading to the veranda for breakfast, I think about how normal everything appears on the surface. Seeing the waitresses smiling their welcome, I wonder about their stories. Does everyone here have a sorry tale to tell? Are we all a carbon footprint of the next in line? Everyone seems young and impressionable and even the older staff doesn't have many years on us. There must be a fast turnaround because we all appear to be the same age. That fact alone strikes me as weird and so I'm surprised when I head into the kitchen and find an older man barking orders at the busy staff who appear rushed off their feet.

He sees me hovering nervously on the edge and barks, "What!"

It makes me jump. "Um, I was sent to arrange the guest's welcome and leaving requirements."

He looks angry and growls, "We are in the middle of service. Does anybody around here understand what that means?"

I am shaking in my canvas shoes because he looks so ferocious, and I don't miss the pitying glances thrown my way by the kitchen staff. He shouts across, "Adam! Deal with this."

I'm relieved about that because I instantly hate this chef magician on sight.

He turns away and Adam races over, rolling his eyes, which makes me giggle. He whispers, "Come on, let's get out of his way."

He draws me to the side and says with concern, "Are you ok? That was a lot to take in last night."

"I think so."

I try to smile. "I still can't believe it."

"I wish it wasn't true, but there are too many things that can't be explained."

He grabs a notebook from a hook on the wall and says with a sigh, "Ok, what do you need?"

"Whatever the guests need to take when they check out and the welcome package for the incoming ones."

He writes it down and then lowers his voice. "Nate was in earlier."

"He was?"

My heart starts thumping at the mention of him and Adam whispers, "He ordered a picnic lunch. I'm guessing it's for the two of you."

"He did?"

I feel a little anxious, and Adam looks concerned. "I expect he's going in for the kill." His face falls, probably because I turn as white as the dress I'm wearing and gasp, "Not literally, I hope."

His lips twitch. "No, it's a standard seduction technique around here. He'll probably take you to the retreat. It's the nature reserve on the other side of the island. Guaranteed to get you in the mood and lower your defences."

"Are you serious?"

Now I'm extremely worried and it doesn't make me feel any better when he laughs softly. "Relax, there's not a lot he can achieve in a lunch hour, but I'm guessing he'll be wanting to cement your partnership before meeting with his father later."

"Why?"

He says in a low voice. "Because that's Nate's job. To get you on side and indoctrinate you in our ways."

"You make it sound like a cult."

"Maybe it is."

My eyes widen and he raises his eyes. "Think about, Katrina. They make weird appear normal. They make you believe that this is acceptable behaviour, and you start to accept this is how life is. There's a reason they recruit impressionable teenagers who have suffered trauma. They give you the world and change theirs forever."

"I still don't understand why?"

I'm conscious that we're taking longer than we should when I see the chef's irritated gaze fall on us and Adam must get the vibes too, because he snaps the notebook shut and says as an aside. "I'm guessing the answer lies in those meetings Chester arranges with the guests. I just need to work out a way to listen in."

He moves away with a loud, "All done. Catch you later."

As he heads back to his station, I walk away with this fresh information, adding more confusion to the pile already waiting to be sorted into some kind of order. There appears to be a lot wrong with Catalina Island and now Adam has brought it to my attention, I feel more afraid than ever.

17

Diana is on her break when Mr and Mrs Barker-Smythe check out. I look with interest at the middle-aged couple who appear tanned and rested as they say their goodbyes.

"I hope you enjoyed your stay."

I smile pleasantly and Mrs Barker-Smythe sighs. "I wish we had longer. It was paradise. I don't think I'll ever top this vacation."

Her husband looks lovingly at his wife. "It was everything we hoped it would be."

"I'm glad. Perhaps we will see you again one day."

For some reason, they look surprised and Mrs Barker-Smythe looks anxiously at her husband. "Do you think…"

He shakes his head with a firm, "No."

I'm a little confused, and he smiles. "It will all work out just fine and we will be a little busier in the future."

His wife is positively radiant, as she says with a slight catch to her voice, "I really hope so, Kelvin."

They share the look of a couple guarding a delicious secret and as Chester heads our way, they turn to him and positively beam.

"Chester, thank you for everything."

He smiles as if sending off his own relatives. "I'm so happy everything went according to plan. We'll be in touch."

Mr Barker-Smythe lowers his voice and I strain to hear him, pretending to be reading something in the oracle. "How long before we hear from you?"

Chester guides him away from the desk and I'm conscious of their low whispers. Glancing up, I see a touch of anxiety on Mrs Barker-Smythe's face and wonder if it has something to do with the meeting they had a few days ago, according to the ledger. Obviously, something happened because this is not normal behaviour for departing guests, surely.

I glance at the entries already listed for the next few days and see an entry for Mr and Mrs De Vere, who are meeting with Chester tomorrow afternoon. I am so intrigued by that and wonder if I can somehow eavesdrop. The location is the chat room, wherever that is, and I decide to ask Diana later.

I watch as the couple are led outside by Chester and Nate appears to load their bags on the trolley.

"Hey gorgeous, let me deal with this and then we can grab some lunch. I've got a treat lined up for my favourite girl."

How I wish this was innocent and how I wish we could enjoy whatever this is without the fear surrounding me. I so want to believe that Nate is genuine and hope like crazy that Adam and Matty just suffer from overactive imaginations brought on by too much sun because this is the single best thing that has ever happened to me.

I smile, hoping it blinds him to any doubts in my eyes. "I can't wait."

He winks as he heads off and my head spins with anxiety. I feel as if I'm living in a parallel universe to everyone else and I'm praying that fate intervenes and proves there is nothing sinister going on here at all.

∽

When Nate returns, he brings Diana with him. "Lucky you. I understand you're heading to the retreat for lunch."

"The retreat?" I play dumb and she whispers excitedly, "The nature reserve I was telling you about. Enjoy, and I expect a full report when you get back."

Nate holds out his hand and claims mine in his strong grasp and says lightly, "Your chariot awaits."

"My chariot?" He grins. "You'll see."

We head out into the brilliant sunshine, and I see a golf cart waiting with what appears to be a cooler on the back.

"Wow, I've never ridden in one of these before."

He helps me climb in and winks. "Then prepare for the ride of your life."

Feeling a bit flustered at the suggestive wink he throws me, I'm quiet as we head out of the resort and onto a track that appears to run around the perimeter.

"It's not often we get the luxury of an hour at the retreat."

He says lightly, "Chester likes to keep it as a private space for the guests. Lucky for us, it isn't booked out this lunchtime, so I put our names down."

"Do you have to book nature then, Nate?"

He laughs. "In this case, yes, you do. The retreat is one of the treats the guests get to experience including a private picnic in paradise. Champagne, fresh fruit, and lobster salad are just a few delicacies they enjoy. We set it up for their pleasure, but I'm not going to spoil the surprise. You'll see for yourself."

It certainly feels good speeding along the dusty track while appreciating the deep, lush scenery and getting away from the resort for even a few minutes.

Nate is good company, and despite what Adam and Matty say, I still find it hard to believe they are right. I really need to give Nate the benefit of the doubt and make up my own mind, and so this lunch is exactly what we need. I'm going to listen and form my own opinion now I know what to look out for and I feel a lot happier when we stop in a clearing and Nate says with excitement, "Here we are. I'll grab the cooler and show you paradise."

It's impossible not to feel excited about that and as I follow him through the trees, I'm looking forward to an hour of fun and relaxation, not to mention the welcome attention of a man crafted from my dreams. Does life really get any better than this?

∽

WE HEAD through the trees and as we step into a clearing, I blink in disbelief and Nate's low chuckle makes me smile. "Beautiful, isn't it?"

I nod, looking around in awe at a scene I never thought was real. A beautiful paradise is laid out like a feast before my eyes and at the centre of it is an amazing waterfall. The roar of the water cascading down a mountain mix with birdsong. The sun filters through the branches of the trees and the lush vegetation provides welcome relief from the midday sun that beams overhead, its rays warming my soul.

My eyes widen when I see a picnic area set up by the lake, with colourful blankets and large parasols on stands resembling a Bedouin tent. Small beanbags are positioned all around and there is a low table laden with a feast for a king.

"But how…" My mouth drops as I register the effort that has gone into this, and Nate says with a smile, "Impressive, isn't it?"

"It certainly is." I head into the clearing and look around me in awe at the surroundings. It feels so special here. So amazing and like nothing I've ever seen before. It's certainly a far cry from my usual experience of nature at the local park in London where I live, and I feel like pinching myself because I am surely dreaming.

I never expected this, and Nate says from behind me, "I wanted to show you just how special Catalina is. Not many people get to experience wonders like this in the world and we are just one of a select few. It's a far cry from real life on the mainland, wouldn't you agree?"

"I certainly would." I'm still taking it all in and gasp, "I've never seen such a beautiful place."

Nate spins me around and, cupping my face in his hands, whispers, "A special place for a special lady." As his lips find mine, I give into the most delicious feeling in the world. Attraction. I can't help it and I can't fight against it. My heart is overruling my head because being so alone in the world makes this impossible to resist.

As Nate pulls me against him and deepens the kiss, the madness follows because I can't deal with anything more than what I'm feeling right now. Is Nate hiding a terrible secret and could my life be in danger if I go against what he wants? None of that seems to matter on this island paradise and I'll deal with it later because I couldn't deny myself this moment of pleasure if I tried.

We kiss like desperate lovers and after a while, he pulls back and rests his head against mine, looking deep into my eyes. "I hope you're experiencing just a hint of how I'm feeling at this moment." His voice is like smooth velvet against my skin. "I'm not sure how this happened, but my feelings are running away with me."

I smile shyly and feel my heart fluttering with a mixture of excitement and fear. I shouldn't want him, but I do. I can't help it and I hate it when he pulls back and nods towards the picnic. "Come on, let's eat. We have so little time, and I don't want to waste this opportunity. We may not be lucky to experience it for a few more weeks and I'm keen for you to enjoy it while we can."

He takes my hand and leads me to the brightly coloured rugs, pulling me down beside him and, as he casts his eye over the banquet laid out before us, he chuckles, "Even the picnics here are five stars." As he hands me a plate of the most exotic looking salad I have ever seen in my life, I say with appreciation, "This is amazing."

I happily start shovelling the food into my willing mouth before he describes what's on offer and he raises his eyes and says with amusement, "I think it's a mixture of shellfish on a bed of leaves with a light vinaigrette."

"Whatever it is, I could happily eat this forever. You are very lucky to live like this 24/7."

"No Kat, *we* are very lucky because this is now your life if you want it to be."

He looks at me with a considered expression. "Do you want this to be your life?"

"I don't *not* want it to be my life." I sigh. "But how? I'm only here on a temporary visa after all, and reality beckons. Luckily, Madelaine was around to help when I needed it most, but she can't change what's happened."

"Do you want to talk about it?" He looks concerned and it would be so easy to open up to him, but I'm conscious of the red flags waving all around me where it concerns him, and I smile to disguise my anxiety. "Maybe some other time. I don't want anything to ruin this special moment. What about you? What are your plans for the future?"

He takes a bite of a club sandwich and shrugs. Once he's finished, he looks into the distance and says in a lost voice. "I just want to feel as if I belong somewhere."

"I understand that feeling."

He smiles and I can't stop staring because if this man is a cold-blooded killer, I'm Cinderella.

"I found out who my real father was on my eighteenth birthday." He looks so sad my heart tightens as he sighs. "Not such a great present, really."

"Eighteen sucks, if you ask me." My voice is sharp, reminding me of my own experience of eighteen, and he sighs. "It does. My mother told me I should know who my father was. I was surprised because I always thought it was her husband who died when I was a baby." He puffs out a deep breath. "Obviously, I had many questions and to her credit, she answered every one. My father, as it turned out, was just a one-night stand. That didn't make it any easier."

Thinking about my own parents and how much in love they were, I feel his pain. "What happened next?"

He looks angry as he says tightly, "I asked if she knew where he was now. I mean, I had questions that needed answers, and you may be surprised to discover who that man is."

My heart thumps as he opens up to me and he sighs. "It's Chester Monroe."

I say nothing and just stare at him in surprise, and he shakes his head. "She just slipped me his phone number and told me I should arrange to meet him. I asked why now? I mean, if she was in contact with him, why leave it until my childhood had gone?"

"That's a reasonable question."

He says bitterly, "My mom changed before my eyes that day. It was as if her guard lifted and the bitterness that lived there spilled out because she was so angry. She told me I was his problem now; she had played her part and if I wanted to know the reason why he wasn't around, I should ask him. She wanted nothing to do with him, or me, as it turned out."

"You must be wrong. You're her son."

I'm shocked at his story and feel angry on his behalf, and he turns away, making me reach out and grasp his hand.

"Don't hold it in, Nate. You're allowed to be angry and bitter about this. It's not you who's in the wrong here."

"I know." He stares at me, looking quite lost and now my mind is filled with a different feeling towards him.

"So, what happened next?"

"I called the number." He exhales sharply. "It felt odd calling my father on my eighteenth birthday for the very first time in my life. He was a stranger; someone I never knew existed, thinking my real father had died before I even got to know him. I suppose I'd accepted I'd never know what it feels like to have one and I was in shock. I was experiencing so many emotions and didn't know what I was feeling at the time. Anger, bitterness, and pain. Resentment and curiosity. It's hard for any child growing up with only one parent, but a guy needs his father just as much as a mother and the fact mine was on the end of that call was a huge moment in my life."

"It must have been." I squeeze his hand and he shifts a little closer. "We arranged to meet up as if we were arranging a business meeting. He told me he'd send a car that afternoon and to pack a bag. He would explain everything when we met and not to judge him until I knew the facts."

"That was incredibly brave of you. To meet him so soon after you learned the truth."

"I had no choice; you see, my mom was packing my bags as I was speaking to him."

"Why?" It seems so cold, and he says bitterly. "She changed the moment she told me. It was as if she couldn't wait to see the back of me. It hurt so much. At that moment, I felt rejected twice over. My life was suddenly built on sand, and I didn't know who I was anymore."

I edge a little closer and put my arm around his shoulder because it seems the right thing to do under the circumstances. Whatever Adam and Matty think of Nate, nobody could fabricate the emotion in his voice, and I feel so sorry for him.

"So, I loaded my bags into the car that arrived within the hour and turned my back on the woman who had meant everything to me. I never said goodbye – I was too angry. She didn't even stick around to watch the car leave, which hurt. It was as if she couldn't wait for me to leave, and I still don't know why." He exhales sharply. "Anyway, I was taken to the airport and found a seat with my name on it to Miami and another car picked me up and, like you, I was met on the dockside."

"Your father." He nods.

"It was obvious who he was. We looked so alike. The moment I saw him, I knew this wasn't just a sick prank my mom thought up for my birthday."

"You really thought that."

I'm shocked and he laughs bitterly. "I thought of everything to explain the madness. I tried to think of an excuse why she was being so cruel and, as it turns out, she had none. She *was* cruel. At that moment, she wasn't my mother. She was lost somewhere in the past when a mom doesn't live up to the job description and her child makes excuses for her. There were many times she looked at me with a strange look in her eye and I suppose it was the fear of this day ever happening. I'm not sure why it took my eighteenth birthday to make her decision, but it was as if she couldn't live with the guilt anymore."

"How do you feel about her now?" I'm curious because if I was in Nate's position, I'm not sure I could forgive that easily and obviously neither can he because he says angrily. "Maybe one day I'll go and find her but right now, I'm happy to never see her again."

He grips my hand hard and lifts it absentmindedly to his lips and kisses my fingers before saying, "Chester turned out to be everything I wanted in a father. He brought me to Catalina and spent time with me. Told me that he had paid my entire life to make sure I had everything I needed. The reason he was absent from my life was because my mother wanted it that way. They had come to an agreement that he would stay away, and the choice would be mine when I became an adult."

"So, she was honouring that agreement."

"Apparently so."

"Maybe that's why she was so cold. To protect her heart. I can't believe she wasn't completely destroyed when you left. It can't have been easy."

"No, it wasn't."

He sighs and looks a little guilty. "I'm sorry, Katrina, I ruined this special treat with a dark tale. We'll talk about it another time, but I wanted you to know because of tonight."

"Tonight?"

"Dinner with my father, of course. Madelaine is back later, and Chester likes us to dine as a family when she's here. He also said she asked to meet up with you because she was worried about how you were coping."

"She's very kind." I owe Madelaine a lot, and Nate nods. "She is. She's not here much, and I know Chester misses her like crazy. If any couple gives me hope for my own future, it's them."

"What makes you say that?"

"Because they're living the dream. Don't you think?"

"Not really." He looks surprised and I say slightly wistfully. "When I fall in love, I wouldn't want to be apart from my husband for any amount of time. From what I see, they have it all but each other for most of the time."

Nate laughs. "Some might say that's the best kind of relationship there is. They don't have time to get bored with one another and look forward to the time they do have."

Thinking about Adam's tale of Chester's wandering eye, I wonder if Nate is deluding himself because if Chester and Madelaine have this amazing relationship, it's built on lies and adultery and that is definitely not something I want in my future.

18

I must glide back into reception with the look of the besotted because Diana grins when she sees me coming. "I see the retreat lived up to its reputation."

"Is it that obvious?"

She leans on the desk and says in a low voice, "Well?"

"What?" I grin impishly and she rolls her eyes. "How did it go? Did you move your relationship on and if not, what's the matter with you?"

"We talked."

"I sincerely hope that's a euphemism for something else." She groans, making me laugh.

"No, really, it was nice."

"If that's how you get your kicks by, um, talking, then good for you."

Shaking her head, she says quickly, "Anyway, I'm desperate for a comfort break. Are you ok to hold the fort here? I've checked in the new arrivals already. Mr and Mrs DeVere. Extremely posh and dripping in designer brands. I hated them on sight."

"That's harsh." I laugh as she shrugs. "One day I'll check in here as a guest. I've got ambition, you see, and if I don't meet a super-rich husband here, then I'm relocating my search."

"Is that why you're here?"

I'm a little surprised, and she laughs. "Bien sûr, ma chérie, je ne me contenterai pas de moins que ce que je mérite."

"Your French is coming along well."

"It certainly is, and to be honest, I am so relieved."

"Why?"

She winks and taps her nose. "All will be revealed at the opportune moment. Wish me luck."

She heads off and I think about Diana. She appears to have everything worked out, and I wonder what her plan is. She definitely has one, and as soon as she returns, I'll question her some more.

Now I'm alone, I cast my eye on the oracle and start flicking through the pages. It appears that Catalina Island is always relatively full, if you count occupancy of twelve rooms as full capacity.

They could fit so many more in and I wonder who devised their business plan. The fact they enjoy the best food, drink and facilities tells me it isn't cheap, but some of these people don't look as if they have the sort of money that's required to check in to such a luxurious resort.

I jump out of my skin when a deep voice behind me says, "Are you finding everything you need?"

I look up and see Chester smiling at me. Hoping to God I don't look guilty, I say quickly, "I was just familiarising myself with things. How many guests you usually have, how long they stay, that kind of thing."

He moves beside me, and flicks open the book and says pleasantly, "Do you have any questions?"

Swallowing my guilt, I say quickly, "I was going to ask Diana about the meetings in the chat room. It appears that all guests are booked in for that and I wasn't sure how it works. I suppose I'm just curious in case any of them ask me."

I'm babbling a little and he nods, seemingly not put out at all by my question.

"Call it a welcome chat. You see, Katrina, our guests are not the kind who enjoy a package holiday and travel en masse. They require a more bespoke kind of holiday and it's up to me to find out what their expectations are. As the general manager, it's important that I welcome them all personally. Not always when they first arrive, but certainly within a couple of days."

He points to the latest entry, Mr and Mrs DeVere. "They are booked in tomorrow after breakfast. They need to unwind first and unpack and then once they've had a chance to settle in, I can tell them what's on offer. Standard procedure in most resorts."

I feel a little stupid now, thinking it was something more sinister than that and now I'm second guessing everything I heard last night. This can't be anything more than above board and I'm sure Matty must have got the wrong end of the stick when he spied on Nate through the binoculars. Chester also seems normal and quite charming, and I'm not sure I want to associate with Adam and Matty anymore, filling my head with stories of wrongdoing and murder.

Chester smiles. "I'm looking forward to our dinner tonight."

"Yes, Nate told me. I hope I'm not intruding on your family time."

"Not at all. It will be good to get to know you."

He looks concerned. "So, how are you settling in? It can't be easy after what you've been through."

"It's fine. To be honest, it came just at the right time. I was lost after my… well, what happened and on top of that, losing my home was brutal. I'm just glad Madelaine rescued me and offered me this lifeline. I am so grateful."

"That's good to know." He looks thoughtful. "What about when the six weeks end? Have you thought any more about that?"

"Not really. I suppose I'll save my wages here and rent a room in the college. Get a job at the local pub or supermarket to pay my way until I graduate."

"What do you want to do?"

"Medicine." I feel my face light up. "I've always wanted to help people and luckily seem to achieve the grades required. It seems a good fit."

Chester looks thoughtful. "Maybe you should take a year out. Let the dust settle and spend it here. We could extend your contract."

"Really." I'm surprised because I never thought of deferring before. "But I only have one more year of my course left. I should at least finish that."

"I'm not saying you won't. I'm just saying maybe you can study it remotely." He leans against the desk and smiles. "I like to encourage learning here, Katrina. Most of the time the staff have time on their hands, and it could get tiresome for them. So I allow studying during the day. Diana studies French when she's not occupied with business. Nate is studying further math with a view to accounting and Sven is doing a teaching degree. You could finish your course remotely and then study medicine online. Put in the groundwork at least, which will make it easier when you move on."

He smiles kindly. "You're young and there is no rush to do everything now. Take some time and a deep breath. A lot has happened to you lately and it would be good to take a moment and reflect. This is the perfect place to do that, so think about it."

He looks at his watch. "I should go. Madelaine will be arriving shortly, and I need to be on the dock to welcome her home. Think about what I've said, the offer's there."

As he heads off, it strikes me that there was nothing weird about that conversation at all. In fact, it all made perfect sense and now I'm even more confused than ever. After last night's rendezvous, I thought I was in Bates Motel. Now, in the bright sunlight of the day, I feel like a fool. Maybe I should reserve judgement and collect the facts because my imagination is running away with my common sense, and I need to get a grip.

～

IT MUST BE thirty minutes later that I look up and see Madelaine Covington walking towards me, holding Chester's hand. They are laughing together as Nate wheels her cases behind them.

She looks up and throws me such a sweet smile I think I fall in love with her. She is certainly impressive. She was both at the funeral and when I met her in town. Super stylish and oozing confidence. A woman who makes the effort in all aspects of life and her immaculate appearance, perfect make-up and styled hair make it look as if she's stepped fresh from the shower, not an aircraft.

"Katrina, how lovely to see you. I hope things have settled down and you're feeling happier now."

"Thank you. This is an amazing place."

She smiles, revealing a perfect set of veneers which makes me feel shabby and unworthy in comparison.

"I hear you've hit it off with Nate." She laughs softly, and says in a stage whisper, "I may be biased, but he's the greatest guy on this island."

Chester pulls a face and coughs, which makes her laugh. "Other than you, darling, of course."

It's a little embarrassing as he lowers his lips to her eager ones, and they share a very inappropriate kiss while Nate rolls his eyes and gags behind them.

It makes me giggle and as they pull apart, Madelaine blushes adorably. "Sorry, what must you think of us? It's just that we really miss one another when we're apart."

She looks lovingly at her husband, partner, I'm still not sure what they are, and Chester smiles. "Come on, we need to be alone."

I don't know where to look and Nate grins at my obvious discomfort and whispers as they leave, "Cringe. Do you think they realise that?"

"I don't think they can think of anything but each other."

"And you, Kat, what are you thinking?"

He leans on the desk and looks deep into my eyes and, to be honest, I can't think of anything but him right now.

"Work." I laugh softly as I flick the book in his face. "So much to learn, so little time."

He pretends that I've wounded him and staggers away with a

loud, "I'll give you something much more interesting to think about tonight. I promise you that."

He heads off with a cheeky smirk and once again, I push the doubts away. Murdering psychopath? I'm just not feeling that right now and as I return to my investigations, it's with a huge smile on my face.

19

Chester and Madelaine live in a small bungalow on the edge of the resort and as I walk there hand in hand with Chester's son, I feel a little nervous. It's one thing dining with the other staff, but this feels so different because of who they are.

Nate is also uncharacteristically quiet, and I squeeze his hand. "Are you ok?"

"I'm fine." He sighs. "It's just that I prefer it when we're alone.

These dinners are hard to endure sometimes because of their high expectations."

"Like what?"

Now I'm worried and feel like something the cat dragged in when I think of my charity shop dress and flip flops.

"They are so high powered, so driven. They expect everyone else to be the same. I always feel as if I need a lie down after an evening in their company and I'm worried I'm a disappointment to my father."

"I doubt it, Nate. You're amazing."

He laughs out loud. "You are my favourite cheerleader, Katrina. I'll need you to hold that thought because after tonight, you may think differently."

I'm curious and say nervously, "Is Madelaine ok about the fact Chester's your father. It must have come as quite a shock."

"She's fine." He smiles. "Madelaine's great in every way. I don't think anything shocks her. She just accepts it and moves on."

I wonder if there are any more sons or daughters in the shadows and can't help asking, "Does he have any other children, or Madelaine perhaps?"

"A few."

"A few!" I'm stunned, and he laughs slightly bitterly. "They don't live here, but he showed me some photographs. A half-sister who lives in Monaco and a half-brother who is a whizz with computers and landed a great job in Silicon Valley. There are the twins who live in Germany and the sister, half of course, who lives in New York and is about to be married to a very wealthy man."

"Nate." I'm so shocked I just gasp his name and he shrugs. "It appears my father is quite free with his favours."

"And Madelaine, does she know?"

"She does and doesn't seem to care."

"Wow, that's very liberal of her."

He shrugs. "They're a strange couple and you must hand it to them. They certainly live for the moment and I'm guessing Madelaine is no saint when she's away either."

"What about her? Does she have any children?"

"A few I believe."

"A few! For goodness' sake, Nate, this is weird."

He looks sad and I feel bad for him. "I don't want to be like them, Katrina. I want to fall in love with one woman and spend my life with her. Make a family and raise them with love. Maybe one day I'll leave Catalina and find it on the mainland, or maybe it's here all along."

The intense look in his eyes burn through to my soul and I feel a shiver pass through me as he appears to be searching for answers.

"I'm sure it will happen one way or another." I try to make light of an increasingly tense situation, and he grips my hand a little tighter. "Maybe it already has."

We walk in silence the rest of the way because I have no words and neither does he, it seems. He has laid his cards on the table, and I wonder how I feel about that. Should I allow him in, or slam the door in his face? I'm too young and inexperienced to know, but something still feels strange about this whole situation and I need to learn more before I agree to anything.

∽

Chester's house is amazing and if I thought the guest's bungalows were impressive, they are nothing like this.

We head through a large white door into chic elegance I have only seen on television programmes about the super-rich. Marbled floors and white silk curtains, abstract art and modern furniture, make this house serene and luxurious and just the large white sofa and deep pile rugs make me feel as if I'm in paradise.

The man himself watches us approach, and I see why he's so popular with the ladies. His white linen shirt hangs open, and he is wearing low slung trousers that look as if they are made of silk. The designer black stubble on his face is the only rough thing about this man and his obsidian glittering eyes watch us approach with a great deal of interest.

"Come in and grab a drink." Smiling, he hands us both a flute of champagne each and I feel self-conscious as I stand feeling very much like the hired help amid such elegance.

Before he can speak, however, a vision wafts into the room and I openly stare as Madelaine drifts in wearing a white silk maxi dress with her blonde hair piled Grecian style on the top of her head. The jewellery hanging from her throat and wrists is elegant and tasteful and her nails look professionally manicured, both on her fingers and toes. She even has a silver toe ring decorating her tiny feet and I wish I had made an effort more than anything right now.

Chester hands her a glass, and she smiles lovingly into his eyes.

"Thanks, darling, it's good to be home."

She heads across to the sofa that's facing the view, providing the perfect vista through bifold doors leading onto white decking where a private hot tub is bubbling away.

Curling her legs underneath her, she sits with her hand resting on Chester's knee and she rubs it absentmindedly.

"So, Katrina, I hope you've recovered after the shock of the will. Such a terrible thing to happen."

"It was." Leaning forward, I say eagerly, "Did you find out who this company is?"

She nods. "Yes, The Green Valley Foundation is perfectly legitimate. It survives on many similar donations and uses the money for charitable purposes. You may not like hearing this, but it was a very honourable thing your parents did in donating their money to such a worthy cause."

"It doesn't feel honourable from where I'm sitting." They raise their eyes, and I don't care about that because charity begins when the basics have been taken care of and leaving me with nothing has scorched my soul.

Nate places his arm around my shoulder and pulls me against him. "Of course you'd feel like that. It's understandable."

"I wouldn't worry, Katrina." Chester's smooth voice sounds like a calm breeze through a hot, scorching wildfire. "You have us now and we will be happy to take care of you."

"Of course." Madelaine smiles. "You are the perfect addition to our island family and who needs money when you live like a queen on other peoples?"

She laughs out loud and Chester grins, clinking his glass with hers. "True enough. The guests pay for paradise and we live in it. It's why Madelaine's job is so important."

"What does that involve?"

I'm curious, and she leans forward, her eyes sparkling. "I'm the saleswoman and the ambassador selling this place to people who can afford it. I travel the world promoting our private island and keep a steady stream of visitors coming through those doors."

I'm still a little confused because surely that would cost more than they make and she must sense that because she smiles, looking as if she's indulging a small child who can't grab simple multiplication.

"I'm not talking about normal people, Katrina. These are people who crave something different. Usually, we are recommended, and I follow up leads. Mix in their circles and befriend them. One customer here is usually worth at least ten more as they recommend it and then their friends recommend it. I scour the world for eligible people and make sure I choose my guests carefully. One day I'll show you how it's done if you like. If you decide to make Catalina your home, of course. After all..." She smiles up at Chester lovingly, "I may want to ease off a little and spend more time here. It will be good to have a successor I can share the job with."

As I think about the possibilities and look with envy at their lifestyle, I find myself being sucked deeper into this amazing world they have created. What's not to love about it? It's the perfect life and they are living the dream, and with Nate beside me, I could imagine myself firmly wearing Madelaine's shoes. It's an option I never even considered, but one I'm keen to explore further because out of pain and misery, a future is unfolding that I would be a fool to turn away from.

20

Dinner is like everything on Catalina – five stars. I'm surprised when Joseph, the head chef, arrives to cook our meal and I actually see him smile at something Chester says.

Madelaine is easy company and after a while says, "Let me show you around, Katrina. Nate can spend some time with Chester."

Nate nods. "Of course, have fun."

We head out of the huge open plan room and Madelaine sighs. "I love being home. It makes everything worthwhile."

"It must be hard leaving this."

She nods, looking wistful all of a sudden. "It is. It's not just Catalina either. It's Chester and Nate, of course."

I'm curious about what she thinks about that, and it must show in my expression because she throws me a long, considered look. "You're wondering about Nate and Chester, aren't you?"

I feel a little uncomfortable, and she smiles ruefully. "Chester adores me. He always has, but in the past, he had a wandering eye, which when you see how we live, explains it a little."

She leads me into a huge bedroom, and I blink in disbelief because this place is designed exquisitely and is the largest space I have ever seen with a bed in it. She sits on the edge of it and pats the space beside her and as I do as she says, I wait for a story that may make things a little clearer.

"When I first met Chester, it was in a business capacity. It must have been over twenty years ago, and he was in his prime. I was intrigued by him. He was so self-assured, so charismatic, and when he brought me here and showed me how amazing it was, I fell in love and not just with him. This life is a narcotic that hooks you almost immediately. He directed so much attention on me I was smitten. I was much like everyone else here at the time — lost. My parents sold our childhood home and moved to another state and I was in a spot of bother."

She smiles. "So, you see, Katrina, we are all the same. Lost and looking for a place to belong. Rejected and left by our parents with all the confusion that brings. Chester fills that void and offers us a new beginning."

It all sounds so noble, and I feel a little foolish for believing the sinister tales, but it still doesn't excuse his wandering eye when she's not around, and I wonder if she knows about that.

"When we became partners, I was the happiest girl here. He told me about his past, girls that he partnered with, children he had. I knew he had a chequered past, and he has always been upfront about that. How could I judge him when I had done the same?"

I stare at her in surprise, and she nods, looking a little sad. "I enjoyed my teenage years a little too freely. I suppose that's why my parents were keen to get rid of me. I was a wild spirit with no moral compass. When I came to Catalina, it was as a rebellious young adult and Chester showed me a different way."

"Does Chester own Catalina then?"

She makes it seem as if he's lived here forever, and she laughs softly. "Now he does, but back then it belonged to a man named Grady Anderson. He was Chester's father and a very charismatic man, like his son. You know, Katrina, I see a lot of you and Nate in Chester and me. You're a little younger than us when we first met, but I recognise similarities, which makes me happy."

She lowers her voice. "Nate hasn't been here that long and is still adjusting to finding out that Chester is his father. The fact he was partnered with Darcey who subsequently left, made him doubt everything for a while. I see a difference in him already, and it's only been a few hours. You focus his mind and settle his heart. I did that for Chester back in the day. He needs me and I need him. Surely that's true of everyone, isn't it? We all need a port in the storm and someone to hold us when life deals us a wild card. A best friend and lover with only our best interests at heart. Someone who knows you inside out and adores every part of you. That's what I have with Chester, and I see that same look in Nate's eyes when he looks at you. It may be early days, but I see it as clear as that ocean out there. It was destiny mixing with fate that brought you to Catalina and I'm hoping you decide to make this your home. It would certainly make us happy."

It's a powerful speech and I can see why she is so good at her job attracting guests to the island. I would agree to anything in this moment as she smiles at me with honesty and sincerity brimming in her beautiful blue eyes. I don't think I have ever met a woman like Madelaine Covington in my life and if I could choose a role model, I doubt I'd find a better one. Then there's Nate. So perfect and everything I look for in a boyfriend. It would be so easy to stay. To turn my back on my old life that I left tattered and bleeding in the gutter when I left. Step out of madness into serenity. That's how it feels at least, but I can't shake the huge black cloud following me that formed after my conversation with Adam and Matty. Casting doubt on this perfect paradise and letting the devil inside my head.

She appears to be waiting for me to say something, so I just smile and say breezily, "I have fallen in love with Catalina and this life already. I could well do the same with Nate, but I'm a little guarded because my heart is bruised and not really functioning right now."

"I understand." She grasps my hand and squeezes it with empathy and says sweetly, "Stay as long as you need to find yourself again on Catalina. This life is amazing and if anything, takes away all the worry many live with. You have food, a beautiful place to stay and purpose in helping run an island paradise. Then you have love. Not just from the most amazing man on the planet either, but from everyone who shares this life with you. From one person without a family to speak of, to another, welcome home."

Suddenly, I'm carried along on a wave of possibilities. I would be mad to leave. For what? Pain, misery, and worry.

Chester said I could study here and why not? I would be a fool to leave and so I nod and say, "I'd like to stay."

Her face breaks out into a huge smile, and I'm surprised to see tears in her eyes before she hugs me close and squeezes me tightly. "I'm so happy for you, Katrina. You have made the right choice. A life-changing one and it would be our pleasure to look after you, keep you safe and give you a home."

It's a little overwhelming because now I've made that decision, it's as if a huge weight has lifted. I feel so free. The worry just melted away and Madelaine pulls back and strokes my hair like a proud mother and smiles. "I'm so happy for you, darling. Embrace life on Catalina and enjoy everything it gives you and who knows, one day you and Nate will be Chester and me. I can recommend it."

Thinking of Nate leaves me with a warm feeling inside. I could have it all. I can see that clearly now and as she takes my hand and shows me around an island paradise, it just reinforces my decision even more. I want this, I want Nate and I want to be Madelaine in the future. Who wouldn't because she is living the dream?

~

EVERYTHING HAS NOW CHANGED and as I spend the evening with my new family, I'm a great deal more relaxed than before. Nate is attentive and sweet, and Chester and Madelaine are good company and make me feel like one of the family as we spend the evening drinking amazing cocktails while relaxing in their luxurious home. Joseph prepares us a banquet in honour of Madelaine's homecoming, and I don't think I've ever been as happy as I am now. It feels as if a huge burden has lifted from my shoulders and I'm able to breathe again.

It's almost a wrench when it's time to leave and as I say my thankful goodbye, I know I made the right decision.

Nate walks me home and as we stroll hand in hand, he says, "You seem different tonight, Kat. More relaxed, happier even. It's good to see."

"I feel good." It surprises me how good I do feel about my decision and say happily, "I think it's this place. It works its magic and draws you in."

"That's annoying."

"What is?"

He nudges me playfully. "I thought it had everything to do with me."

"Maybe just a little." I grin and his low laugh drives away the final traces of doubt clinging on. We reach my room, and he leans against the wall and pulls me against him, burying his face against my hair and sighing with pleasure. "This is the part I hate. Leaving you."

My heart is thumping a little louder and my head spins with decisions. It would be so easy to invite him in and cement our relationship in a more intimate way. The trouble is, it's a huge leap of faith for me because I'm not *that* girl. I'm not one to sleep around. I never have, so this is a very big decision for me. Deciding to leave that particular battle for another day, I pull back, smiling shyly. "It's late, and it's been a long day."

He nods. "Of course. One last kiss, though." His cocky grin crashes through my shaky defences and I say shyly, "I'd like that."

Kissing Nate is a delicious act of indulgence. Something I want and yet know will inevitably lead further at some point. I can't help myself. His attention is like a drug. It's new and exciting and different from anything I've ever experienced before. I've never been so desired, so pursued and I know it's only a matter of time before I take the next step with him, but not tonight. It would be too much on top of my decision to stay. The alcohol making my decisions for me in a haze of happily ever after is not the best plan of action. Will it be the final page in a fairy tale? I'm still not convinced of that, so as I enter my room alone, I turn my back on the next step of my dream.

21

The week passes in a haze of activity. Madelaine is like a breath of fresh air through the resort and brings a certain level of excitement with her. The guests are happy to see her, and the staff seek her out, craving her company and keen for some of her shine to rub off on them. I wonder how she does it. She's so charismatic and I am no exception. I love spending time with her and feel kind of special when she seeks me out and invites me to share a coffee or a walk along the beach.

For the most part, we talk about Nate and the island, but often she talks about my parents and encourages me to unburden my grief.

Nate also seems happier and more relaxed, and they spend more time together as a family.

Then, on the fifth day of her stay, my bubble bursts.

I'm working on reception when a couple of guests stop by.

"Good morning. It's a lovely day." I smile my greeting and note that the woman looks a little on edge and her husband is nervous.

"We are booked in for a chat with Chester at eleven. Can you tell us where to go?"

"Of course." I smile and wonder why they look so worried and try to put them at ease. "I'll show you. It's not far."

Placing the bell on the desk to alert the back-room staff if somebody needs help, I accompany them to the chat room that is situated behind the spa.

In the distance, I see Katie apparently lost in thought as she gazes off into the distance and feel bad that I haven't spent much time with her this week. Along with Diana, she has become a firm friend and so I decide to ask her to meet me for lunch today for a catch up.

We reach the chat room and, like everything else on Catalina, this room is furnished with luxury in mind and is a light and airy room overlooking the mountain. The sun filters through the shutters and creates an oasis of cool calm in a hot tropical paradise.

"Please take a seat and I'll arrange some refreshment. Chester won't be long."

The woman looks around nervously and I wonder why because what on earth does she have to feel nervous about?

I make to leave, and her husband says suddenly, "Are you

happy here?" I look at him in surprise and find them watching me intently as if my answer matters a lot and I say with a smile, "Yes, it's perfect, amazing actually."

"Where are you from?" I sense an interest that goes way beyond politeness and say carefully, "London, England."

The woman smiles. "I could tell from the accent."

They share a look. "How old are you?" I feel as if I'm under a microscope and shift a little on my feet, suddenly desperate to be anywhere else but here.

"Eighteen."

"You're very young." She almost looks disappointed about that, and I smile, feeling a little on edge at the considered looks they are throwing me.

"Do you study?" Her husband is keen to carry on his line of questioning and I nod. "Yes, I'm studying hard because I want a career in medicine one day."

I don't miss the look they share, almost as if they've made a decision between them. Then the door opens and Chester breezes in like a jet of water putting out a fire because for a moment there it felt a little intense.

"Mary, Brad, you're looking nice and rested. I hope the room is to your liking."

"Perfect, thank you."

Chester looks at me and smiles. "Thank you, Katrina."

Taking that as my cue to leave, I hear him say, "I have ordered us some refreshment. I'm sure you will appreciate a cocktail to help you relax."

As I close the door behind me, I wonder about them. Why do they need to relax? It's as if Chester saw how on edge they were and was taking steps to reassure them. My curiosity burns as I walk away and then I see Drew carrying a tray of brightly coloured cocktails towards the chat room.

He smiles as he sees me. "Hey, Katrina, you're looking particularly lovely today."

He laughs when I roll my eyes. "You're such a flirt, Drew."

Winking, he makes to pass, and I say impulsively, "Would you like me to take them?"

He looks surprised. "Would you? I've got a few guests waiting and it would help, if you're sure it's no trouble."

"Of course."

As I take the tray, I feel a little foolish because I'm not sure why I offered, really. Maybe it's the part of me that hopes to hear a little of their conversation because I'm still none the wiser about what these chats involve. Nobody seems to know and yet the guests always appear thoughtful when they leave that room and I've always been curious about things that shouldn't concern me.

Strangely, my heart thumps as I approach the chat room and I hesitate in the doorway. The door is slightly open, and I hear the gentle murmuring of hushed conversation and strain to hear. It's annoying though, because I can't make out a word and with a sigh of frustration, I head inside with a smile.

Chester looks surprised to see me carrying the tray. "Oh, Katrina, I was expecting Drew."

"He had some guests waiting, and I offered to help."

He smiles. "Thank you." Standing, he retrieves the tray from my outstretched arms, and I catch Mary's eye as she smiles kindly.

"Thank you, Katrina." Chester turns away, effectively dismissing me and I head to the door and as I close it behind me, I hear Mary say, "What about her?"

There's a pause in the conversation and it's so frustrating to leave because what have I got to do with anything?

Something isn't right and I hesitate on the step, wondering if I can somehow listen in and then I spy a window that appears to be slightly open and feel my heart thumping as I inch my way around the building and crouch down low outside.

I hear Chester's low drawl wafting through the partially open shutters. "She's new and not ready yet."

Mary sounds disappointed. "But she's perfect, beautiful, clever and personable."

"I'm sorry, you know I like to help as much as I can, but we have a procedure here and she's further down the line on that. No, here is the perfect one for you."

It is so tempting to stay but I'm conscious if anyone came around the corner, they would catch me listening in and there is no reasonable explanation about why I'm crouching beneath an open window, so reluctantly, I head back the way I came, not any further forward in knowing what goes on inside that room.

As I pass the spa, I decide to pay Katie a visit and as I head inside, I take a deep breath of the intoxicating aroma that always calms my spirit.

It's always darker in here, more serene. A tranquil escape from the heat of the sun outside and as I enter, Katie looks up and I'm surprised to see her pinched expression and worried eyes that are quickly disguised with a smile.

"Katrina, to what do I owe this pleasure?"

She changes her expression, but I know something is wrong, so I say breezily, "I wondered if you fancied meeting me for lunch. It would be good to catch up."

She nods. "Sure, what time?"

"What's best for you?"

She consults her appointment book. "I have Mary booked in after her chat. That will take me to twelve-thirty. What about one o'clock?"

"Sure, I'll let Diana know."

As I make to leave, I turn back and say casually, "Do you know what they chat about?"

"Who?" She looks confused. "The guests and Chester. I still don't know and I'm curious, I suppose, because I've just delivered them cocktails in the chat room."

She shrugs. "I don't know but..."

She beckons me closer, and I quickly head her way and lean in as she whispers, "Don't ask questions about the chat room, Katrina. Chester doesn't like it when the staff start snooping around. For some reason it makes him angry."

"How do you know?"

She sighs. "Jenny was the same as you. Curious. She started asking questions about the running of Catalina. She seemed worried about something and wouldn't let it go. I saw Chester pull her aside one day, and they didn't know I was watching, and things appeared quite heated. The next day she left."

I have an uncomfortable feeling about that, and she sighs. "I really liked Jenny. She was bright, good fun and seemed to really like Adam. I'm not surprised he was upset when she left with no warning because I'm sure he would have gone with her if he had the chance. Whispers around the resort are that Chester asked her to leave. The fact she never left with her belongings tells me it was a sudden decision."

"That's so strange. Why would she leave without her things?"

"We're not sure but Darcey was told to pack them up and they would be sent on. The next thing we know Darcey also left."

"With Jenny's things?"

I'm so confused, and Katie shakes her head. "No."

She looks sad. "Nate was like Adam for a while. A little lost and then you arrived, and he changed almost immediately. I think he really likes you."

Thinking of Nate, I feel a prickle of happiness but there is something about life here I'm just not sure about.

She straightens up and clears her throat. "Anyway, I should prepare the room. I'll see you later."

I head back to reception, a thousand thoughts crowding my mind. My earlier happiness is being edged out by my doubts and I can't shake the feeling that something is passing me by unnoticed.

Diana is back from her break when I return, and she appears to be learning French again as I see her mouthing words with her headphones in.

She sees me coming and removes them, smiling brightly.

"Hey."

"Hey." I join her behind the desk. "Sorry, I just took the latest visitors to the chatroom."

"No problem."

"I stopped by the spa on my way back and I said I'd meet Katie for lunch at one. Is that ok with you?"

For some reason Diana looks thoughtful. "How did she seem?"

I look up sharply and see a concerned look in her eye.

"I'm not sure; a little distracted perhaps."

Diana looks around and leans in, whispering, "Matty told me Sven's worried about her. Apparently, she's withdrawn, and he's fearful she's going off him."

"It happens I suppose."

"Of course, it's just that she's been acting strangely for a few weeks now."

"Do you think we should ask her if everything's ok? Perhaps she needs someone to talk to."

She nods. "Maybe you should test her a little over lunch. She may confide in you."

"I don't want to pry though."

Diana shrugs. "I don't think it'd be prying. Just ask her if she's ok and see what happens. We all need someone to talk to and she's a quiet one."

"Possibly."

She replaces her headphones and I think about what she's said. There is so much hiding under the surface on Catalina and I'm keen to start unravelling its secrets and Katie may just be the one to help me with that.

22

I wait anxiously for Katie, and on the dot of one, she appears looking a little tired. She drops into the chair opposite me, and I'm surprised to see she's just helped herself to a yoghurt and bowl of soup instead of the amazing salad that we all usually enjoy.

"Aren't you hungry?" I nod towards her plate, and she shakes her head. "I'm not feeling so good. To be honest, I think I'm coming down with something."

I feel relieved, hoping it's just a cold or similar, and she sighs, pushing her plate to the side and plastering a fake smile on her face. "So, how are things going with Nate? You look happy."

"It's fine and going well as it happens."

"I'm glad."

"How about you and Sven?"

I watch her closely and a little of the light dims in her eyes, making me say quickly, "What's wrong?"

"Nothing. It's just..."

"What?"

I'm determined to get her to open up to me and am surprised to see the tears building in her eyes as she whispers, "I feel so bad, Katrina."

"Why?"

She looks as if she's carrying a huge burden on her shoulders, and I'm alarmed when a tear splashes onto the table that she brushes angrily away. "I'm such a fool." She looks so upset, I lean in and whisper, "Do you want to go somewhere more private and talk about it?"

It's as if I've given her a lifeline and she nods miserably, "Can we?"

"Of course, we can go to my room if you like."

The relief on her face tells me this is the right thing to do, and we quickly leave the canteen and head the short distance to my room, where we can talk without fear of being overheard.

It doesn't take long and as soon as we head inside, she bursts into tears, making me even more alarmed than before. Guiding her to sit on the bed, I place my arm around her shoulders and say with concern, "What's wrong?"

"I'm such a fool." Her words are laced with regret, and she sobs. "I thought I was special."

"You are. What makes you think any different?"

"I just know."

Wondering if she's fallen out with Sven, I say softly, "Did you and Sven have an argument?"

"Kind of."

"It can't be that bad." I smile reassuringly. "What was it about?"

A fresh burst of tears follows, and her shoulders shake as I try to comfort her and then she shocks me by saying, "Please don't hate me, Katrina?"

Now I'm feeling lightheaded because why would she say that unless...

My thoughts immediately turn to Nate and an icy feeling grips me. Does this have anything to do with him? My heart thumps as I try to get it under control and I say nervously, "Why would I hate you?"

"Because of your relationship with Nate."

I say tersely, "Does this involve him? Has he done something?"

"No." She looks up in surprise. "Of course not. I would never..."

Then she sobs again and says in a broken voice, "Who am I kidding? I am exactly that person."

"Please, Katie, just tell me what's happened?"

My mind is running away with all the possibilities, and I just need to know for my own sanity, and her voice cracks as she sobs, "I was having an affair with his father."

"Chester!" I look at her in horror and she nods. "I thought he really liked me. He flattered me, paid me compliments and flirted with me and I loved the attention. It was like a drug. He may be older, but he's still an attractive man and not a boy. It started the day he came to me for a massage. We were flirting - a lot and started fooling around a little. Well, it led to other things and soon the massages turned into something more intimate."

"Oh, Katie." I feel so sad for her, and she sniffs. "He made me think I was special. That he really wanted me. We used to meet during the day in the spa when the place was empty. It was so easy to lock ourselves in the room and if anyone came in and saw him, they wouldn't think anything of it because everyone knows he loves a massage. I suppose I got carried away and soon Sven noticed I was a little cooler around him."

"Does he know?" I can't begin to imagine the trouble that would cause, and she shakes her head. "No, he knows something's not right, but he's just trying a little harder. He's being so sweet it just makes me feel even worse and now Madelaine's back, Chester doesn't want to know me again."

"Do you think she suspects?"

"No. I mean, Madelaine is always so sweet and kind, which makes it worse. She's so lovely to me, and Chester obviously adores her. As soon as she returns, he's all over her like a rash. Then she leaves, and he picks up the next toy in line when the favourite one isn't around."

"Do you feel second best?"

"I *am* second best." She appears angry. "I asked him if he would ever leave Madelaine and he laughed. He told me he loved her, but it didn't mean he didn't care for me." She drags in a harsh breath. "I was such a fool because I believed him. I still do, to be honest, which is why it's so hard watching him with her."

"But they are a couple and maybe you should respect that and concentrate on Sven."

I'm not sure what madness is filling her brain right now and feel a little angry if I'm honest. Then she shocks me by saying in a dull voice, devoid of emotion. "I'm pregnant."

The words hang in the air while I process them, and I look at her in shock as she smiles bitterly. "Chester's baby."

"It could be Sven's." I certainly hope it is for her sake, and she shakes her head dolefully. "We always use protection. That's how stupid I am, Katrina, because I'm so careful with Sven, but let the madness in with Chester."

Thinking about Darcey and how similar this is, I'm worried for Katie and her lip trembles as she whispers, "I told Chester, just before Madelaine returned."

"What did he say?"

"That he would sort everything and not to worry."

I feel a little relieved about that and smile. "He'll do the right thing, but what about you? What do you want?"

"I want him, I suppose. To raise our child together and be happy. I told you I was a fool."

"You're not a fool." I smile kindly. "Just in love."

"That's why I'm a fool."

"Love makes fools of the lot of us, and I'm starting to believe that we'll do anything for it."

"He wants to send me away to have the baby." Her words drop into the conversation like a cluster bomb.

"Where?" I'm shocked and look at her in horror as she brushes the fresh tears away. "He told me Madelaine knows of a place I can go where I can have the baby and no questions will be asked. Then I can return here and carry on, or I can start again somewhere new, and he would help me."

"What did you say?" I feel bad for her because from the sounds of it, Chester has no intention of doing anything but covering up his mistake and she shrugs. "I don't know. It's all so scary. I want to stay here, be with him, and have his support and love. But there's Madelaine."

"She obviously knows then." I look at her in horror and she nods. "Chester told her. It was awful, Katrina. I went to their house yesterday and felt like such a fool. Madelaine and Chester faced me together and told me how unfortunate this was, and they were sorry it happened to me. Madelaine was so good about the whole thing and tried to make me feel better, which made it worse because of what I did to her. Chester didn't even seem guilty and just dealt with the facts."

"Where are you going?"

"To some friends of Madelaine's who are happy to take me in and help me through my pregnancy."

Sighing, I take her hand. "I feel bad for you, Katie. Maybe you should discuss this with Sven."

She pulls back and looks scared. "He can never know. Please promise me you'll tell no one about this, not even Nate."

"Of course. You can trust me."

She looks anxious. "I have a lot to think about and the priority is making sure this baby doesn't suffer. I'm prepared to do what I must to assure its future before I can even think of my own. I must trust Madelaine and Chester. They know what to do and I am just a silly, infatuated girl who let her heart run away with her."

She sighs heavily and stands, looking out across the ocean with a thoughtful look on her face.

"I think I'm going to take Madelaine's friends up on their offer. Take some time out and re-evaluate my life plans. It's the right thing to do. They have money, a lot of money, and Madelaine said I would be treated like their own daughter?"

I'm not sure what I'm thinking right now and yet Katie needs a friend, not someone judging her, so I smile reassuringly. "At least it will give you time to think away from here and the problems that bring. What will you tell Sven?"

"That I'm leaving. That I'm keen to take a job on the mainland and need some space. I must leave soon before the baby starts showing, and he suspects because I can't keep a thing down right now and he's not stupid. He'll put two and two together and make a baby, and then there will be trouble in paradise."

She sighs heavily. "I should be getting back, but thanks, you've really helped."

"Have I? it doesn't feel like that."

She nods with a small, sad smile on her face. "I was a fool, Katrina. Just don't hate me for that."

"I don't hate you, Katie."

She nods and turns to leave with a soft, "Thank you. It means a lot, and thanks for listening."

As the door closes behind her, I'm left with an overwhelming feeling of sadness. The same story from the one I heard before, but with a different victim this time. It appears that Chester Monroe has a huge problem. An addiction that results in children dotted all over the place and in the middle of that is Madelaine, who appears to stand by and support him through the pain. The trouble is, when will it end and what will happen to my friend because this could destroy her, and I feel so worried about that.

23

On my way back to reception, I see Adam heading back along the path and he stops and throws me a searching look.

"Are you ok?"

My confusion must show on my face, judging by the look in his eye, and I shake my head. "I'm not sure."

He looks worried and says quickly, "Listen, we should meet up tonight, same place."

"Is that wise?"

I'm thinking about all kinds of bad things right now and he nods firmly. "Now is the perfect time. I have some news."

"You do?"

Thinking of my own news, I know I'll probably tell him, despite having assured Katie to the contrary. I'm feeling a little out of my depth here and hope I can count on Adam to help me see things more clearly.

He says in a low voice, "Keep it to yourself; we'll meet at ten."

I watch him head off and feel apprehensive about tonight. Things are escalating and I'm not sure how I feel about that.

～

For the rest of the day, I am alone with my thoughts. Diana is happily learning French and I must admit she's pretty good. After a while, I ask her about it, and she smiles. "I chose to learn French for a very good reason. I want to live there."

"You do?" She nods enthusiastically. "Ever since I went there as a child on a family vacation, I fell in love with the place, the people, and the language. My mom and dad encouraged me and told me I could apply for university in Paris. It was all set and then at the last minute they told me there was no money left to send me there and if I wanted to go, I would have to work and earn it myself."

"That must have come as a shock."

"It was a huge shock. We used to have everything, you know. Lots of money, fancy vacations, and fast cars. I had a huge allowance and was spoiled like a princess. Then on my eighteenth birthday, everything changed."

"I'm sorry. What did you say?"

"My birthday."

She shakes her head sadly. "We lost everything overnight. My father made a business deal that went wrong. We had to sell our huge house, cars, and anything of value. Mom was depressed and my father had to look for work elsewhere. They found a live-in job at an estate in Beverly Hills and told me they weren't allowed to take me with them, so I came here."

"That was lucky. How did you find out about this job?"

She smiles. "Madelaine Covington. Apparently, she was a friend of my mom's from college and they kept in touch. She arranged for my position here and I'm working on my dream. My wages are being saved to send me to university in Paris, although it will take a few years to get enough together. When I do, I'm going to study fashion and set up home there. I've got it all worked out."

My head is bursting with so many possibilities, and everything I've heard today is suffocating me. It's all too coincidental. The staff recruited tell much the same story. Then there's Chester's wandering eye and extensive family. Eighteen seems to be the magic number around here and I am connecting dots that reveal a sinister picture. In the middle of it all is Madelaine, so sweet, innocent, and caring, caught up in the centre of everything it seems. It's as if the mist is clearing and I see what's out there because if this private island isn't hiding a terrible secret, then I must be descending into madness.

~

THE DAY PASSES SLOWLY, and I'm counting down the hours until I can discuss my thoughts with Adam and when Nate stops by on his way back from the beach, he is like a ray of sunshine in a dark, gloomy room.

"Hey, baby, how about I take you out for a blast on the boat? You must be dying to escape for a bit."

"Great." I smile and don't even think about it as I head off with excitement to change out of my uniform. I feel happy to pull on shorts and a t-shirt and meet him on the beach inside twenty minutes and he looks so tanned, handsome, and safe as he watches me head towards him with a huge smile on his face.

"I've been thinking about this all day. I can't wait to be alone with you away from this place. It's just what we need."

"We need?" I arch my brow and he grins. "Some alone time. Don't get me wrong, I love this place, but its charms can wear thin after a while. Madelaine has the right idea and mixes it up a little. She gets all the good of Catalina and then the best of life on the mainland."

He helps me into the boat and jumps in after me and as I take my position on the seat behind him, I say thoughtfully, "You could do that. I mean, perhaps you can take over from her and share the sales job. It sounds interesting and I'm sure you'd be a natural."

He shakes his head. "No, that's her speciality. Chester's is managing the resort and the business and mine is to learn from the master."

"What do you mean?"

He turns and I see a look enter his eye I'm not that comfortable with. Hard, bitter, and resigned. He sighs heavily. "Chester wants me to take over one day. Run the business and make sure it continues to thrive. He has big plans and is coaching me about what that involves. There's a lot that goes into this business behind the scenes and I need to escape sometimes."

"Do you want to talk about it?" He looks so upset, it's impossible not to be alarmed at that, and he shrugs. "Maybe one day, but for now I just want to forget. Come on, let's have some fun."

He winks and then eases the boat away from the dock and we are soon blasting out to the open sea. I can see why he likes it so much; it's exhilarating and as we move further away from the shore, it feels as if we're the only ones left in the world.

Soon, he cuts the engine, and the silence is all around us as we bob gently on the turquoise sea, alone at last.

Nate sighs with relief and strips off his t-shirt and I can't help but admire the sight before me. Tanned, strong and muscular, a vision of manliness and kryptonite to a young girl curious about the opposite sex.

He smiles rather wickedly and says, "You can strip off if you like. Nobody will see you."

"I couldn't." I'm mortified at the thought, and he laughs before removing his own shorts, revealing absolutely nothing underneath but what nature gave him. I feel so shocked, and he laughs as if it's the funniest thing he's ever seen.

"Relax, Kat, I'm just going skinny dipping. You can join me if you like. Wear your costume if you feel more comfortable. The ocean is so refreshing, and you will love it."

I must admit I am feeling a little heated, and as he dives into the crystal-clear water, I strip down to my bikini and perch on the edge of the boat. "What happens if we lose the boat?" I call to him as he bobs a short distance away, and he shouts. "We won't."

"How can you be so sure?"

"Because I know this place. We're surrounded by a sandbank and if it drifts, according to the wind direction, it will just end up on the sand. Look."

To my utter astonishment, he stands up and I blink hastily when I see him naked and the water glistening on his toned body.

"Come and join me. It's fantastic."

Feeling the spirit of adventure gripping me hard, I dive into the sea and love the cool water, calming my heated skin.

When I surface, Nate is beside me and to my surprise he pulls me towards him and kisses me deeply and with so much passion it lights a fuse inside me that runs away with me.

His strong arms wrap around my body, and I give into something I have wanted for some time and as he pulls me closer to the sandbank, I leave my inhibitions on the boat.

Pushing me down onto the sand, he carries on kissing me and soon his hands start wandering. The fact we're alone in the middle of the ocean making out in a more serious way, makes none of this seem real somehow. I can't help myself and as things get heated, it melts my common sense and, as one thing leads to another, I push my doubts aside and allow nature to take over because I couldn't back out now if I tried.

24

What have I done?

I sit on my bed and stare into space because now I'm back in my room, I am faced with the consequences of what just happened. I had sex with Nate. Unprotected sex with a man I want more than anything. What if...? Images of Katie sitting here earlier flood my mind and think of myself, possibly in her position. I was so stupid. One moment of lust and madness could ruin my life.

It felt so right, though. Nate was perfect – he *is* perfect and couldn't have been more loving. Even afterwards when he held me close and told me he loved me. He was so tender and concerned. I felt good about what we did all the time we were away from Catalina. Then we returned, and it hit me hard. I could be pregnant. What the hell have I done?

Nate walked me back to my room, and I pretended I was happy. I am, I was - happy. Then why do I feel so afraid?

When I showered, it was with Nate soaping my body. When he dried me and kissed me all over, I felt like the luckiest woman alive and when he took me to bed and made love to me all over again, I loved every minute of it.

We ordered room service, and it felt so good. It was the right thing to do until he left. He told me he had his workout with Sven and would see me tomorrow. I was to get some sleep because he wanted me to be fresh in the morning.

Now I'm left alone with the repercussions of my actions, and I feel like such a fool for giving up something that deserved more thought.

Pulling on my running shoes, I head out onto the path, jogging with my own thoughts as awkward company as I head to the gazebo on the edge of the rocks.

I feel ashamed of myself. I let myself down and I blink away the tears as the fear takes over because what if I'm pregnant? I'll be sent away like Katie and my life will be ruined forever over one stupid moment of madness that decided my fate.

I feel my heart thumping as I approach the edge and sit with my legs dangling over the side, waiting for the signal to jump.

The sound of the ocean is like soothing antiseptic on a wound, and I love how it can do that. It will be fine. I must hold onto that thought because I'm not going to know for quite some time, anyway. There are no pregnancy tests on Catalina and the thought of dealing with such a huge life changing moment is making me break out in a sweat. I'm such an idiot, a lust driven, crazy, stupid, fool, who should have known better.

A firm hand grips my ankle and I jump down onto the ledge and as he guides me along it and into the cave, I feel so foolish when Adam looks at me with concern.

"Were you crying?" I feel the tears wet on my face and almost can't look at him, and his strong hand forces my chin up to look into his eyes. The soft brown eyes filled with compassion undoes me in a way I wasn't expecting and my face falls as the tears flow. He pulls me hard against him, his strong arms wrapping around me like the strongest shield.

"What happened?"

He pulls back when the sobs subside, his question hanging in the air between us.

"I'm so stupid, Adam."

He brushes my tears away with his fingers and says gently, "Whatever's happened, you're not a fool, Katrina. This island messes with all our minds and leads us to do things we struggle to live with."

I look up in surprise and see the twisted look of bitterness he had when I first met him.

"Why, what have you done?"

"A lot of things I'm not proud of, which is why I'm keen to end this madness."

He pulls me beside him on the floor of the cave and whispers, "Chloe told me she overheard the new guests talking when they returned from their chat. She was cleaning the bathroom, and they walked in, not knowing she was inside."

He laughs softly. "Rather than tell them, she listened for a moment and heard the woman say, 'I really hope it works out. Just think, we could be parents this time next year if Chester finds us a willing partner.' I told you something was off about this place."

A sinking feeling hits me as all the dots connect and I say with a hitch to my voice, "They run a surrogate service, don't they?"

Adam exhales sharply. "I think they do. It makes sense when you think about it. We need to know the facts, so I'm going to take a chance and I could use your help."

"What do I have to do?"

"We need to get into his office. There are no computers on the island and no files, just those infernal books he insists on us using. I'm guessing it's a different story in his private office, so I need to get inside and take a look."

"How?"

I'm shocked and worried about that, and he says in a low voice. "I have a plan that's not very honourable but desperate times require foolish actions."

"What is it?"

He says darkly, "There's a reason why Joseph prepares Chester's meals personally."

His eyes shine. "He's got a nut allergy—a serious one. So, my plan is to lace a little peanut oil on his food, and he'll be forced to leave and get help on the mainland."

"But that could kill him."

I'm shocked and not happy about Adam's plan at all. A sinking feeling hits me as the picture begins to focus and I say with a hitch to my voice, "They're selling babies. They must be."

Adam exhales sharply. "It doesn't make sense. I mean, it could be nothing, so I'm going to take a chance and I could use your help."

"What do I have to do?"

"Bring your phone and help me photograph any evidence we find. Keep watch for anyone coming and if we're caught, we can pretend we're having an affair."

"But then what? How will we deal with what we find?"

Adam winks. "Leave that with me, but we must be quick. I have a feeling things are heating up around here and this could be our only chance."

"What makes you say that?"

"I hear the guy's talking. They're angry about the way Chester hits on the female staff. Matty was talking about it with Drew and Sven when I walked in yesterday. Apparently, Sven's been having issues with Katie, and they think it's because of Chester."

"What will they do?"

Adam shrugs. "Who knows, but it's a pressure cooker waiting to explode. We need to find out what's going on, for everyone's sakes. If we find nothing, then we just carry on knowing we have overactive imaginations and accept this place is paradise after all. If we discover something more sinister, then we can alert the authorities and set us all free."

Thinking about Katie, I whisper urgently, "Katie's pregnant with Chester's baby."

Adam hisses, "Fuck, are you sure?"

"She told me today. She said Madelaine knows and has arranged for her to live with some friends of hers until she gives birth. That they will look after her and make sure she has everything she needs."

"Then we have our answer."

"It could be just a coincidence."

"It could, but I doubt it. I'm guessing that is one baby heading to a new home after having been ordered like a toy in a catalogue."

"Do you think so?"

I feel frozen inside and not just because of the damp cave.

"Can you think of a different explanation?"

In my heart I know he's right and now I'm potentially in the same situation, I know I must do everything in my power to unravel this mystery.

We spend the next thirty minutes discussing our plan and decide that it needs to be tomorrow because Madelaine will be leaving the next day. For our plan to work, we need them all to go to the mainland. Adam tells me it takes twenty minutes to get there where they will take him to a hospital. Even if Nate comes straight back, it will take him another twenty minutes, so he calculates we'll have just under an hour, if not more. The staff are due at the social evening, so it will be easy to slip away and search the bungalow. If we're caught, we'll say we had too many cocktails and pretend to be having a fling.

As the plan is cemented in place, I feel a stirring of excitement at the thought of finally getting the answers I know are here somewhere.

When I leave Adam and start jogging back to my room, I take a deep breath of fresh air and hope his plan works. The more time I spend here, the more it takes over me and I'm losing all sense of normality as each day passes.

25

I'm not sure how I get through the next day. I'm on edge the whole time because so many things are running around in my head right now. Everything seems like a smoke screen. The smiling guests who appeared so innocent before, now feel like vultures circling. I look at each one of them and wonder why they're really here. Then there's Nate. Carrying on as normal and throwing me suggestive looks when no one else is looking, promising a repeat performance of yesterday. I'm still torn between my feelings for him and it's confusing me.

Diana appears to be the most clueless of everyone. Just enjoying her work and learning French on the side with her dream firmly intact. Katie looks as miserable as I feel and the men of the resort have angry eyes and pained expressions, which tells me there is a storm building that could decimate the island.

Nate stops by at lunchtime and leans on the desk. "Let me rescue you and take you to lunch."

He stares at me with such a caring look, I almost believe he loves me. He has given me no reason to doubt his feelings and part of me wants to believe he's genuine.

We head off and he places his arm around my shoulders and kisses my head, whispering, "I missed you last night."

Immediately, I tense up because what he if he came looking for me and wondered where I was?

He laughs. "Sven told me my mind wasn't on it last night and he was right. I think that was the longest hour of my life and he pushed me hard, but I wasn't feeling it. I just wanted to be with you."

"That's nice." He laughs. "I hope you mean the part when I wanted to be with you and not the way he pushed me to breaking point."

"That you missed me, of course." I nudge him playfully, and he grins. "We're good together, don't you think?"

"I think." I smile into his eyes and look for any sign that he's not genuine, but there's nothing there but happiness, which makes me feel a little better.

He whispers, "Madelaine's leaving tomorrow, and they want us to dine with them tonight before the party."

"They do?"

He nods and looks so happy I feel bad because it's like I'm a double agent or something. A spy in their camp and it's not a nice feeling at all.

We meet up with Katie and Sven, who are obviously struggling for conversation due to the stony looks on their faces and the awkward silence in the air.

They look relieved when we join them and Nate says cheerily, "So, how are my favourite couple?"

"Good, thanks." Sven nods, but it's obvious he's unhappy and Katie offers a small smile. "Good, what about you? You seem to be in a good place." She looks at me with a curious smile and I blush a little, making Sven roll his eyes. "Nate strikes again."

"What do you mean, again?" Nate's voice is sharp with a hint of warning in it and Sven says bitterly, "The golden boy. The one who drifts through life with everything coming easy to him."

I stare at him in shock as Katie says sharply, "For God's sake, Sven, cut it out."

Sven grabs a beer and drains the can, squeezing it in his hand before banging it sharply on the table. "I'm leaving."

Nate jumps up and runs after him and Katie sighs. "I'm sorry about that, Katrina. He's been in an impossible mood all day. I think he suspects."

"I'm sure he does." I feel sorry for my friend, but he doesn't deserve this either and I feel so much sympathy for the guy who obviously loves her very much.

"I'm leaving tomorrow." She sounds so sad I instinctively reach out and grip her hand. "Does he know?"

"No. It's best this way. Chester told me I could leave with Madelaine in the morning, and she would make sure I was settled in my new home."

"Won't that feel strange?" She looks up and shrugs. "If you mean that my lover's girlfriend is making sure I'm ok, despite the fact I'm carrying her boyfriend's child, I'd call it extremely strange."

I don't know whether to say anything or not because I wonder how much Katie knows, so I say carefully, "Will you come back when it's over and do they even allow children on Catalina?"

Katie leans forward and hisses, "Wake up, Katrina. I won't be back, it's obvious. Where on this island is anyone who's left before? I'll be replaced with another gullible fool, and I'll be taken care of, making sure their secret is safe."

"What do you mean; what secret?"

"Work it out and open your eyes. Girls leave here all the time and never come back. First Jenny, then Darcey and now me. You could be next because there's a reason why they choose vulnerable girls with no family to speak of. We're disposable. Less likely to have questions asked about them and I've been told they'll set me up in a new life if that's what I want in return for my silence."

"They said that?"

My eyes are wide, and she nods, looking so angry I'm worried about her. "Don't be me, Katrina. Get out now while you can before you end up like this. There are no happily ever afters on Catalina Island. No gold pot at the end of the rainbow and no treasure beneath the sand. We are used and then disposed of. Just don't make my mistake and work out a way to get off this island, because the only way you can leave is if they allow it."

She stands abruptly and says over her shoulder, "If I don't see you again, good luck. It's been nice knowing you."

She brushes past Diana, who looks a little shocked as she carries her plate of food across and sits down with a gasp. "Wow, she's angry. It must have something to do with Sven. I saw him pushing Nate outside and then Drew arrived and pulled them apart. What's going on?"

"I don't know." I don't want to drag her into this mess because I'm convinced that she is one of the innocent few on this island. The fact she's partnered with Matty makes me think she's better off than most because they appear to stay out of the drama and appear happy. I almost envy her a routine that apparently works for her. Work, learning and a cocktail on a sun lounger at the end of the day. Diana has it all worked out and Matty appears to be doing a good job of looking out for her and if anything, it gives me hope that the rest of us are just reading sinister things into a perfectly reasonable explanation.

∼

JUST BEFORE SEVEN, Nate knocks on my door, and my heart flutters when I see him standing there. He's wearing beige shorts and a white polo shirt and looks freshly showered and smells like a dream.

"Looking good honey." He bends his head and kisses me lightly on the lips and everything feels so normal I could cry. I want this. I want him and I want what we have to be real. Not part of a sinister plot to ruin people's lives in return for making another person's dreams come true. It all sounds rather farfetched when I think of it now and as we walk along the path towards Chester and Madelaine's bungalow, I push it all aside and concentrate on spending a pleasant evening while I pretend everything is just fine.

Madelaine opens the door, looking chic in a white silk dress with sparkling sandals on her petite feet. Her long blonde hair is swept into a messy bun on her head and her startling blue eyes brim with warmth and welcome. Like the fairy godmother in most fairy tales, Madeleine is the person who can make all our dreams come true and I want to be like her. Loved, chic, gorgeous and kind. She is beautiful inside and out, especially because she tolerates being with a cheater.

Chester smiles his usual smooth grin, and I will myself to smile back. I am fast falling into hate for this man but owe it to Madelaine and Nate to try to tolerate him.

"So, I'm leaving again tomorrow for three weeks."

She smiles at Nate. "Make sure the boat is ready at 10 am. I'm taking Katie with me, so they'll be two sets of luggage to place on board."

She sees my expression and smiles. "Katie has decided to leave Catalina, and I set her up with a fresh start somewhere else. Such a lovely girl; she will do well."

Keeping my voice even, I say airily, "What's she going to do?"

She doesn't skip a beat and smiles. "Be a nanny for a family I know. They were looking, and she mentioned she needed a fresh start, so I put them in touch. I do so love helping people. It makes me happy."

Chester pulls her against him and drops a kiss on her perfectly made-up lips. "I love you, honey. You are everything I want to be."

"Oh, Chester–" The look she gives him is full of love. "I'm only this way because you make me so happy. I want a little of that happiness to rub off on the people I care for."

Her eyes find mine and she smiles. "I want this for you, Kat. I have a good feeling about you and Nate. Now you're onboard, I want to spend more time with you when I return. Take you under my wing and show you how it works around here. Chester is doing the same with Nate and we are hoping to offload some of our work to you both, freeing up our time to be together more."

Nate's hand slips into mine and he says softly, "I can't think of anything I'd like more. I'm so happy you came, Katrina. You've made me so happy."

Luckily, I'm spared from answering and we all look up when Joseph, the chef, appears in the doorway. "I've finished up here. It's all laid out and ready."

Madelaine flashes him a blinding smile and says gratefully, "Thank you, Joseph. You always look after us so well."

The surly chef nods, but I see a twinkle in his eye that's not normally present as he stares at the lovely Madelaine.

"Thanks, Joseph. We'll call if we need anything." Chester is quite dismissive, causing Madelaine to roll her eyes and as Joseph heads out of the room, she frowns. "Chester, you should be a little more gracious, especially when he's gone to so much trouble."

Chester shrugs, "I was."

Rolling her eyes, Madelaine grins and says lightly, "Let's head to the dining room. Joseph always pulls out all the stops on my final night."

The table, as always, is decorated beautifully with fresh white linen, tropical flowers and candles. Crystal glasses twinkle beside polished silver cutlery and freshly laundered napkins stand patiently waiting to grace our laps. The lighting is low and the music soft and the candlelight adds a more intimate ambiance to the cosy family meal. Being included in this occasion is a powerful privilege because who wouldn't want to be part of this?

26

We finish the starter of crab cakes on a bed of toasted seaweed with a dressing that is so delicious I would happily eat it every day. The wine is crisp and cold, and the bread rolls soft, and the way Nate strokes my leg and pays me attention, makes me feel like the luckiest girl alive. Chester and Madelaine are good company and tell me stories about previous guests and their strange habits. It's difficult to imagine anything sinister going on here because this family appears honest and open.

I help Madelaine clear away the dishes and then look in awe at the main ones waiting on the side. Madelaine sighs with pleasure. "My favourite boeuf bourguignon. Joseph certainly knows how to cook his way to my heart."

She winks and lowers her voice. "Back in the day, I quite fancied our irascible chef. All the girls love a bad boy, so they say, anyway, and I idolised him." She giggles at the expression on my face. "We may have had a small fling once, but that was before I got with Chester. The feelings are still there though, not in a sexual way, just a pleasant memory that I dust off from time to time and revisit."

Wondering what she means by that, I help carry the meals to the table and note the pleasure in the guy's eyes. "This looks amazing. I'm so hungry." Nate almost falls on the food and we start to eat and then, as soon as the first forkful enters my mouth, I'm shocked when Chester grabs his throat and then spits out his food.

Madelaine jumps up in alarm and her chair falls back and Nate cries out, "His EpiPen, quickly."

I look around in confusion as they spring into action, and I watch in horror as Chester's face swells up before my eyes and he grabs his throat and appears to be having trouble breathing.

"Quickly, Nate, we don't have long. He's having an anaphylactic shock."

Madelaine's in tears as they pull Chester from the room and Nate calls over his shoulder, "Wait here, Katrina, we need to get him to a hospital."

"I'll come too. Maybe I can help."

Nate shouts, "Too much weight in the boat! We need it to go fast."

I watch them leave the bungalow and wonder what I can do to help. It all happened so suddenly, and I'm worried about him.

I look around helplessly and then hear a firm whisper, "Katrina, hurry, we don't have long."

"Adam!" I stare at him in disbelief as he rushes into the bungalow, closing the door firmly behind him. "Quick, take this phone and use it to record what we find."

"But Chester..."

"Is on his way to the hospital."

"But how, what happened?"

Adam grins wickedly. "As I said, there's a reason Joseph prepares his food and it's because of his nut allergy. I just replaced Joseph's olive oil with peanut oil, and we have our opportunity. I knew they would all go with him, but we don't have long. I'm guessing we have one hour before Nate returns, hopefully longer, but we will need to have finished our search and leave no evidence."

I can't believe what I'm hearing but follow him to Chester's office and feel my heart banging out of control. This is so wrong. Why am I helping him? Chester could die. All these thoughts are racing through my head as I look blindly around the organised office and see Adam opening drawers and cupboards like a special agent.

"Hurry, Katrina, help me look." He says with an urgency to his voice that spurs me into action. Frantically, I take the other side of the room and as I look despairingly around a sudden thought hits me. "Check the art on the walls." My voice is strained, and Adam looks up sharply, but does as I say and begins to move paintings to see what's behind them and the third one reveals a safe buried into the wall.

"Bullseye." Adam grins but I whisper frantically, "It's locked. We can't break into a safe."

"Who said anything about breaking in?" Adam smirks as he enters a code and, as it opens, he rolls his eyes. "Matty was right. The guy's an amateur."

"What are you talking about?"

He whispers, "Matty once told me that if anyone ever broke into the resort, all they needed to know was Chester's birthday. Apparently, he has a poor memory, and it's the only code he can remember."

"How does Matty know?" We could win prizes for whispering as we set about raiding Chester's private property and Adam shrugs. "He's the security guard, remember? He has access to information we don't, and it's only when he was drunk one night, he let this one slip."

"What if he catches us?"

"It's fine. I last saw him laughing with the guests. It's the opposite direction to the beach, and I doubt he even knows they've left."

"Some security guard he is." I shake my head. "Does he have any help, or is he the whole security team?"

"There's Grant, but he's making out with Sonia at the retreat while everyone's at the party."

"Isn't Sonia…"

"Scott's partner." He raises his eyes. "You would be amazed at what goes on behind the scenes here, Katrina."

Something tells me I wouldn't and as the door swings open, we stare inside and I blink twice before saying, "What the…"

Adam whistles softly, "Would you look at that?"

There are stacks of dollar bills, neatly arranged in piles inside the huge safe on the wall, sitting on top of some files and a small leather pouch.

Adam reaches in and starts stuffing his pockets with cash and I say in alarm, "What are you doing?"

"We need this."

"No, we don't, Adam, put it back."

He hisses, "Katrina, we don't have long. Get the file and the pouch before they catch us."

"But why? This could be nothing. Why are you risking everything?"

He sighs and thrusts the folder at me. "Look in there?"

My fingers tremble as I open the file and the papers in there don't mean much to me at all, but three words stand out like a gigantic red flag and change everything in an instant.

Green Valley Foundation.

"Adam." My voice shakes and he says quickly, "Now do you understand? We need to run, Katrina, if we're to stand any chance of bringing this organisation down. The money is ours anyway, the guests leave our tips with Chester and he 'keeps it safe' for us."

"But how do you know this?"

He thrusts wads of dollar bills at me and says through gritted teeth, "We don't have time for explanations. Stuff this in your bag. We need to get going."

I watch as he closes the now empty safe and enters the security code. Then he carefully places the art back on the wall and looks around him. "Make sure everything is exactly as we found it. I don't want to give them cause to check the safe until we're far away from here."

I look around, not really registering anything but the fact that Chester is somehow connected to the foundation who now owns my inheritance.

My head is buzzing as Adam says urgently, "Come on."

"Where?" I feel my heart go into freefall as I whisper, "There's no way off the island."

"You're wrong. There's a boat."

"That's on the mainland. How can we escape?"

Adam grabs my hand and, pulling me along with him, says in a loud whisper, "Have you ever ridden a jet ski, Katrina?"

"Are you mad, I'm not going on that?"

"Trust me, it will be fine."

"But we can't just leave. What about our passports? We have nothing and they'll find us."

"We have money, that's all we need. Now hurry, we really don't have time for discussion."

I'm not sure why I've agreed to this, and the only thing pushing me along with him is the folder. The answer to everything lies in there, I know it does and knowledge is what I need right now because I am so close to discovering the secrets of this private island and even though it won't bring my parents back, it will make me understand the connection they have to it.

27

It feels so frightening running after Adam, keeping to the shadows as we make our way down to the beach. We hear the music and laughter coming from the bar and the tears sting my eyes as I make my escape. What am I doing? This seems so wrong. I don't want to leave. I'm happy here. I'm running away with someone who is one breath from madness because Adam has a wild look in his eyes, and the only thing driving me along is my thirst for knowledge.

We reach the beach and Adam leads me to the far end where

a small boathouse sits and hisses, "They keep the jet skis in here. We should really take them both, but I'll take both sets of keys so nobody can follow us."

I watch him grapple around for the keys and my head is spinning with everything that's happening around me.

I can't stop thinking about Nate, though. Surely, he's not involved in anything illegal or immoral. I just don't believe it and I want to cry when I think of what I'm leaving behind. I hate thinking of him returning and finding me gone with all the money and their private stuff. He'll think it was me.

I wish things were different and none of this was happening and I stutter, "Adam, I don't think I can do this."

His eyes sparkle in the moonlight as he says in a loud whisper, "I can't leave you here."

"Why not?"

"They will kill you."

"Why are you saying that? Of course they wouldn't. I really think you've got that wrong."

He hisses, "It's all an act, Katrina. They are cold-blooded murderers, and if they think you know anything at all, they will dispose of you like they did Jenny."

"But you don't know that for sure. You only have Matty's word on that."

"Enough, Katrina. I'll explain everything when we're away from here. Please, just trust me. I'm all you've got."

Something about the fear in his eyes tells me there's more to this than he's telling me and as he pushes the jet ski into the water, he says in an urgent whisper, "Come on, hold on tight, we must be quick."

Fighting back the tears, I wade into the sea and jump on, gripping him around the waist, feeling as if this is a very bad idea. Not just because it's black and scary out at sea, but because I'm leaving Nate. I really like him and don't believe for one minute he's the man Adam seems to think he is, but as Adam fires up the jet ski, I know there's no backing out now.

I don't have time to think as we cut through the waves heading towards oblivion. It feels so frightening as the spray hits my legs and I taste the salt on my lips. My bag is secured around my body, and I hold on tight, shivering in the thin cotton dress and flip-flops that make up the most ridiculous getaway outfit.

Adam is dressed more suitably and had the sense to wear jeans and a sweatshirt, his own bag around his body. Then again, he had time to prepare. I had none and I wonder why he didn't brief me in advance.

I don't look back. I *can't* look back because this feels so final and so wrong. When they return and find us gone along with all their money and files, they will call the police and we'll be hunted like the criminals we are. I still don't believe Adam's right. He *can't* be right because it's so unbelievable.

I'm not sure how long we ride for, it feels like hours but then suddenly, I spy lights indicating we're nearing the shore.

My heart starts thumping with anxiety and I wonder if Adam has really thought this through. Where will we go and how long will it take for the authorities to catch us?

He cuts the engine and whispers, "Jump off. I'll deal with this."

As I wade to shore, I'm surprised when he pushes the jet ski back out to sea with the engine running and runs up the beach. "Hopefully, they'll think we've drowned or something. It's a long shot but may buy us some time."

He grabs my hand and pulls me after him and I don't have time to think as we run at speed up the beach and into the trees.

We reach cover and I'm panting hard when Adam stops and looks at me with concern. "Are you ok?"

"Not really." I am far from ok because I can't believe we just did that.

"Come on, it won't be long, and we'll be able to talk."

"Where are we going?"

"There's a place I know where we can unravel this mystery."

"Is it far?"

"It has to be."

"How will we get there?"

Adam pats the bag he's carrying. "Money."

He stops and takes a deep breath and then whispers, "Ok, we're coming into the light. There should be a cab somewhere around here and we must act like any normal other couple out for the evening."

I swallow hard as he takes my hand and squeezes it reassuringly. "Not long now. Just pretend we're together, and I doubt anyone will suspect a thing."

We head into the light, and I notice we're on a boardwalk where a few people are strolling along, either hand in hand or in groups. It all seems so normal and yet my heart is thumping as I walk into the unknown with a man who scares me a little. Adam seems to have it all worked out, and I think he knows a lot more than he's telling me and as we move along the boardwalk, holding hands like any other couple, I'm guessing we could be anyone in this crowd of strangers.

We must walk for five minutes before Adam says, "Over there, look."

I follow his eyes and see a line of cabs waiting and he says with relief. "Nearly there. Let me do the talking and act naturally."

We join the line and soon reach the front and Adam leans in the window and says casually, "Can you take us to the station?"

"Sure, hop in."

Adam opens the door and I step inside, trying to look as if

I'm on a date or something and as he jumps in beside me, he throws me a reassuring grin and I see the sparkle in his eyes as he sighs with relief.

The cab pulls away and I daren't look back because somewhere back there is a mess that's not going to go away and could potentially ruin my life forever.

∽

We take a thirty-minute ride to the bus station in Fort Myers and hardly speak for most of it. I pretend to be asleep because I have so many thoughts to process, and my head is spinning with what just happened. We reach the bus station and Adam pays the driver and we walk in to buy two tickets to Orlando, and I still can't believe I'm doing this. It all seems surreal, and I wonder if anyone has noticed we're missing yet. As we wait for the bus, I whisper, "Where are we going?"

"We'll take the bus to Orlando; it should take around three hours so we should try to sleep. Then we'll pick up a bus to Jacksonville where the guy that I think can help us lives."

"You think?" I'm not sure Adam's plan is a good one, and he nods. "Yeah, it's a guy from college who loves this kind of stuff. He will be the perfect person to help us because nobody knows my connection to him."

"Which is?"

"I don't have one, which is exactly why he's perfect."

He must see the confusion in my expression because he laughs softly. "Elliott Cohen was a weird guy at college that creeped everyone out. He was into all sorts of computer stuff, and nobody really knew what went on inside his head."

"Sounds scary. Are you sure you can trust him?"

I don't like the sound of this guy, and Adam nods. "He's good. He used to run a side business where students could pay him for information. I believe he set up on his own after college, private investigation via the internet. A modern spy, for want of a better word. If you needed anything finding out, Elliott was your man and I doubt anybody would even think of him in the same sentence as me."

"Do you know where he lives?"

"I know where he used to live, which is a start at least. His parents came from Jacksonville, and I know the house they lived in, so we just turn up there and ask for him. If they've moved, I'm pretty sure we can find out where by asking around in the local diner or something like that."

"It's not much of a plan." I'm feeling even more anxious now, and he nods. "I know, but it's all we've got. Hopefully they won't think to look for us there and there's nothing on us they can track. I'm hoping we've bought us some time at least to get to the bottom of this."

"And then what? What if it's all legal and above board? What do we do then?"

I'm really worried about that, but Adam shrugs. "We head home and carry on rebuilding our lives."

"While being hunted down for theft. We could be arrested and thrown in jail. I'm so worried about this, Adam."

He pulls me in close and whispers, "Relax, nothing is going to happen to us, and we are going to discover the truth."

The bus arrives and as we sink down in our seats, I look out of the window, trying not to draw anyone's eye. I'm shaking inside because I have a bad feeling about this and I'm regretting ever agreeing to leave Catalina with Adam at all.

28

It takes us three hours to reach Orlando and we sleep for most of them and it's only when we board the bus to Jacksonville that I begin to feel as if we may have pulled this one off. The further we get away from Catalina, the better I feel and as we take a seat at the back, Adam whispers, "Let's look at the folder now. There's nobody around us and we have three hours to read up on it."

My fingers shake as I retrieve it from my bag and as we

spread it out on the drop-down table in the seat back in front of us, I look eagerly at the rows of typing.

Adam whistles and points to the names at the top of the first page and we see Chester and Madelaine are down as directors alongside two men. One is called Kent Hawkins and one is Parker Evans.

"Who are they?"

Adam shrugs. "Who knows?"

We carry on reading and note the registered offices are in Monaco and Catalina Island is listed as one of its subsidiaries.

Turning the page, we see rows of entries on a spreadsheet with names, addresses and contact details. The more I read, the more nauseous I feel when I see listed entries in black and white of business deals with vast sums of money neatly recorded beside every entry.

Adam whistles, "Look at those figures."

"This one says $250,000." I point at one entry, and he says angrily, "It's listed as pending. What do you think that means?"

He points to a reference number beside it, and I shake my head. "I'm not sure. Maybe it's on another spreadsheet."

There must be hundreds of names on here and all of them listed with eye watering sums of money beside them and the addresses appear to be from all over the world.

We scan the document for a long time and then my heart starts beating fast when I see a familiar name.

"Adam look." I stare at the page with so much emotion inside, I can't stop the tears from spilling onto the page. "Mr Anthony Darlington and Mrs Marissa Darlington. Are they…?"

"My parents." I swallow the sob that's threatening to draw attention to us, and Adam places his arm around my shoulder and whispers, "I'm sorry, Katrina."

We look at the entry against their name and see the words, "Estate pending, deceased."

"It's so cold." I stare at him in miserable shock, and he looks angry. "Bastards. It's just an entry on the spreadsheet to them. What do think it's for?"

"I'm not sure, but there's a reference number listed beside their name and I'm guessing that information is on one of the flash drives in the leather pouch. I hope so at least." A cold feeling grips me, and I say anxiously, "What if it's all legal and we've stolen their private property?"

I still can't help worrying about that, and Adam shakes his head. "Nothing about this seems legal. I'm guessing Elliot will have a field day with this information, and we need to make sure we have everything covered before we go to the authorities on this. Until then, we lie low and wait for Elliot to do his stuff."

"If we find him and if he agrees. We're not sure of anything right now."

"I am." Adam looks so determined I wonder what else he knows and say quietly, "What made you suspect them in the first place?"

"Whispers around the resort. Snatched conversations and from observing the guests. Jenny used to confide in me and tell me things she heard. She worked in the spa and told me she often heard couples discussing it while they waited for treatments. They thought they were alone, and she used to listen in. Then Matty told me similar things, and I began to watch a little closer. When Jenny disappeared, Chester made a point of spending more time with me. Telling me he'd heard from her, and she was happy working in another resort in Mexico. He tried to make out she had taken a better offer, and they wished her well, but when Matty told me what he saw, it made me angry. That was when you arrived, and I struggled to keep my anger in. Chester pulled me to one side and told me I needed to get a grip, or I'd be asked to leave. He made it seem as if Jenny just left without a thought for me and encouraged me to spend time with Chloe. It was only when she told me of her own fears I realised we had to stick together. That's why I apparently settled down and Chester thought that was the end of it."

"So how is Matty involved? He seems quite happy at Catalina."

"Matty used to drop hints into the conversation. Little pieces of information that got me thinking. After a while, we got closer, and he told me stories of Nate you wouldn't believe."

My heart lurches when he mentions Nate and I say, fearing the reply, "Like what?"

"The boat trip with Jenny, for one. The different girls he takes out on the boat for hours and when they return, the whispers of what went on there."

I feel sick. "Like what?"

"I don't think I need to spell it out for you, Katrina."

"But why would he?"

Adam waves the file in the air and growls, "Here's why. It's not just Chester who keeps the family business going."

"You're wrong." I'm clutching at straws, and he knows it because he lowers his voice and sighs. "I'm sorry, Katrina. Maybe you're the exception. I'm sure he really likes you, but I hate to say it, you're just one in a very long line. Joseph has been there the longest and when he gets drunk, he can be less guarded with his comments. Take Madelaine for instance."

I think I know where he's going with this and he says roughly, "They've been having an affair for years. Meeting when Chester's busy elsewhere. Brief encounters that aren't always discreet. It's not only Chester who likes to sample the staff, but also Madelaine as well. They deserve each other and it's rubbed off on their son."

"You're wrong."

I'm so convinced that Nate's innocent in this and Adam looks worried. "I'm sorry. I'm just telling you what I know. You're not the first girl who's fallen for him and definitely won't be the last."

"But Madelaine said she had a good feeling about me; that she wanted us to follow them in the business."

"It's all lies, Katrina and I hate to be the one who spells it out for you, but Darcey said exactly the same. The next thing she's pregnant and shipped off to one of their 'friends'. It's standard procedure with that family, and you must believe me."

My heart is tied in knots as I battle with what he's saying. I don't want to believe him, but deep down I do. Everything he says has happened to me already and I'm getting an uneasy feeling about events yesterday. Instinctively, I run my hand across my stomach and feel the fear inside. What if he's right? What if yesterday was designed to create yet another commodity for sale? I feel sick just thinking about it and say in a strained voice, "I think I may need to visit the pharmacy in Orlando."

"Are you sick?" Adam looks concerned and I stare at him through soulless eyes. "I may need the morning-after pill."

To his credit, Adam just puts his arms around my shoulders and pulls me close, and as I rest my head on his shoulder, I feel beaten. I'm officially emotionless right now and my head hurts with everything I've learned. Most of all, I need to be sure I'm not another one of Nate's victims and even though it could be pointless, I need to do everything possible to stop this now before somebody else gets hurt.

29

We reach Jacksonville the next afternoon, and I'm exhausted. Adam checks us into the local motel and says apologetically, "I'm sorry we must share. It won't draw attention that way and we need to stick together."

"It's fine." I'm feeling sick anyway and my head hurts, which is probably due to lack of sleep and the fast food we've snatched along the route. But most of all, it's probably down to the pill I bought over the counter at Walgreens – the morning after one. I am tired, sick and wrecked and all I want to do is sleep for the next hundred years.

The motel is basic but clean and Adam throws his bag on the bed and nods towards the bathroom. "You go first, take a shower, and try to relax. I'll leave you to grab some sleep and head out to see if I can locate Elliott."

"Are you sure?" The last thing I want is to go anywhere else, and he smiles. "It's fine. Just don't answer the door unless you hear me call. Ok."

I nod, too weary to argue, and as I take a hot, welcome shower, I try to empty my mind of everything that's happening.

Sleep comes easily when you're on your last shot of adrenalin, and as I fall into oblivion, I'm grateful for the darkness. I'm not sure how long I sleep for, but it feels like forever because when I wake, light has turned to dark, and I feel the heavy ache in my muscles that tells me I've slept deeply. I feel so thirsty and as I look across to the other bed, I'm alarmed to see Adam's bed is empty. He never returned.

Now I'm wide awake and feel the fear clutching at my heart because what if he's never coming back? What will I do?

I quickly pull on my dress, wishing I'd brought a change of clothes and start pacing the small room in worry. I'm thirsty and hungry but daren't leave the safety of the room and it must be an hour later that I hear a knock on the door and a soft, "Katrina, it's Adam."

Flinging the door open, I'm so relieved to see him, and his bloodshot eyes tell me he's exhausted.

I usher him inside and he groans as he falls on his bed and says, "It's done."

"What's done?"

"I found Elliott. He's got the folder and flash drive. He's also given me a burner phone to use. We're to wait until he's had a chance to look at the evidence."

"Can you trust him? What did he say?"

I have so many questions, and Adam groans. "Can I answer them later? I really need a shower and some sleep. I'm running on empty here."

It feels so frustrating, but I know how I felt, and he must be feeling much worse, so I say, "Of course, I'm sorry."

As he shifts off the bed, he says as an aside, "Don't worry, we can trust Elliott. He's still the same geek that he always was." He chuckles, "You know, he wasn't even surprised when I rocked up with this shit. He even wrote me out a ticket for my possessions, as he called them and told me he'd be in touch within twenty-four hours. His rate is fifty dollars an hour, and he obviously does well for himself because he had a gold Rolex on his wrist and a Maserati parked in the driveway. Mind you, he was always loaded so I'm not surprised."

He laughs softly as he heads into the bathroom, leaving me with a thousand questions, desperate for answers. I wonder if we can trust this school friend of Adam's, but I suppose he's all we've got and above all I'm looking forward to hearing what he has to say.

∼

As Adam sleeps, I worry. I think about my parents, Nate, and Madelaine. I revisit every conversation we ever had and try to think back on conversations at the resort that reassure me Adam is spot on with this. I wonder if they discovered we've raided the safe. Perhaps they haven't and Chester is still in the hospital with Nate and Madelaine beside him.

What if Nate returned and discovered I'd left with Adam? He will suspect the worst and think we've run off together. So many things hit me as I lie in the shadows, with only Adam's gentle snores to keep me company. Then I think of my parents and how lovely they were. Did they buy me, are they really my parents and is my life built on a lie?

My thoughts turn to Madelaine and how lovely she is. I just can't imagine her being so cold and calculating. Surely, she's not involved in anything illegal or distasteful.

Picturing my boat trip with Nate, I don't believe he did that on purpose. It was a natural coming together of souls. It certainly felt like that. Adam must be wrong about him – he must be. I'm not sure if I'm trying to convince myself of that because of how hard I've fallen and yet we never used protection. Why not?

So many questions are clamouring for answers, and I soon fall into a troubled, fitful sleep.

∽

WHEN WE WAKE the next morning, we head out to shop for supplies and grab some breakfast. Despite how guilty I feel about stealing the money, I must admit we really need it. We head to a local outlet and stock up on clothes, toiletries, and a couple of small bags to carry it in. Then we shop at the local supermarket and grab water and snacks to keep us going. It feels strange being on the run. We are now criminals and thieves. I'm so conscious of this and can't help looking over my shoulder and jumping at every person, or noise that catch my attention.

We finish up by grabbing lunch at a nearby diner and I begin to feel a lot more human now I've eaten and have some fresh clothes to wear.

"I wonder if they know we've gone." I say for the hundredth time since leaving the island.

"Probably." Adam looks out of the window and says absent-mindedly, "I hope Elliott finds what we need."

"What happens then?" I'm very curious about that, and he

leans closer. "We take it to the authorities. This is too big for us to handle."

"But what if we're thrown in jail? It could all be perfectly legal, and we have stolen from them."

"Then we'll send it to them anonymously and lie low. I don't care how we get it into the right hands, but we need them to investigate, at least."

"I hope you're right about this, Adam, because I'm not sure where to go from here. My passport is back at the island, and I've got nothing but what's in this bag which was bought with stolen money. At least you're still in your own country. In a few weeks' time, my visa runs out and I'll have to ask for help."

Adam looks guilty. "I've asked a lot of you, haven't I? I'm sorry."

"It's fine, I could have said no." I try to reassure him but I'm feeling worried about what this means for me, and Adam says with concern, "Then why didn't you?"

"Because…" I look out of the window and feel the tears burning behind my eyes. "Because I have a horrible feeling about my parent's death."

"In what way?" Adam looks worried and my voice cracks. "It just didn't add up. My father was a good driver. He never took risks and knew that route to town like the back of his hand. He did it often enough and I don't believe for one second he lost control. He always said he'd rather hit an animal that ran into the road than cause an accident and the police officer told me they think that's what happened."

Adam looks concerned. "Do you think Green Valley had something to do with it, then? It's a little far-fetched."

"Possibly, but so is this whole situation. I'm thinking dark thoughts right now, and nothing would surprise me."

We finish up in silence and then Adam's phone vibrates making us jump.

I look at him with a mixture of fear and excitement and whisper, "What does it say?"

Adam lifts his eyes and I see the worry in them. "He told me we're to meet him at the library. In thirty minutes."

"Is it far?" I'm anxious we'll make it in time, and he nods. "Ten minutes' walk."

For a second, we just stare at one another because this could make or break us and I don't know about him, but I'm one very nervous person right now.

30

We head into the library and I'm shaking inside. What if it's a trap and Elliott has alerted the authorities? He may have done. I would in his position.

Adam takes my arm and guides me across the room, and we try to look as normal as possible and not like two thieves in the night.

"He's over there. Act natural." Adam's voice is low and guarded and I almost want to laugh because how is this now my life? I'm a teenager from London who should be partying and studying, not meeting strange men in a library in a place I've never heard of, after stealing from a safe and handing the contents over to be investigated. This isn't my life and I'm not enjoying a second of something that looks so exciting in the movies.

Elliott looks up from behind his thick-rimmed glasses and I see a small weasley man who has zero fashion sense. He has a sharp gaze and a strange look on his face, and I don't like the way he is openly staring at me as if I'm an alien.

We are tucked away in the corner of the library, surrounded by bookshelves, and Adam greets his friend.

"Thanks Elliott, that was quick."

Elliott just smirks. "I wouldn't thank me yet. You've got a huge problem on your hands."

His words cause my stomach to lurch, and Adam turns white under his suntan. Elliott appears unconcerned and taps on his laptop before turning the screen to face us. I try to understand what all those endless figures mean, and Adam asks the same burning question, "What does this tell us?"

"Entries, reference numbers and details of everyone that's ever done business with the Green Valley Foundation." Elliott grins with a look of triumph, obviously enjoying every moment of this. "Some of the entries are marked complete, and the money is cross-referenced to a bank deposit in Monaco."

"Why there?" I interrupt and he shrugs.

"It's where the other directors live, so I'm guessing it's their head office. No tax to pay either, the perfect place to live under the radar."

"Is it illegal?" I hold my breath, not really sure which answer I want to hear.

"If human trafficking is still against the law, you bet it is."

Adam looks triumphant as Elliott continues.

"It appears this is the holding company for an operation that has existed under the radar for generations. I've traced it back thirty years, and that's only when these records were started. The folder appears to be the earlier ones and the later ones are all on flash drives. It appears they sell babies for huge amounts of cash and if the customer can't pay on delivery, they bequeath their assets."

I feel sick and lean back as the room spins around me and Adam says with concern, "Are you ok, Katrina?"

"I think so. I just need a minute."

Elliott shakes his head and pulls up a different tab and says with no emotion, "Mr and Mrs Darlington took delivery of Katrina Darlington on this date. I'm guessing this is your birthday."

He points to the screen, and I swallow hard. "Yes." I blink back the tears as Elliott carries on as if chairing a business meeting. "Debt to be paid on death. All assets transferred to The Green Valley Foundation in return for making sure the delivery is taken care of."

He looks at me with interest. "I'm guessing you were taken care of, Katrina, given the fact you were returned to sender."

"Elliot, please!" Adam sounds angry, and I nod miserably. "So it would seem."

Elliott nods. "I also have contact details for document providers who arrange legitimate birth certificates which name the receiver as the natural parents. In some cases, there are adoption certificates where it makes the most sense and the children are considered legally theirs. None of this has made it through any court of law or registered organisation because I have cross checked some of the entries and they all originate from Monaco."

"So what does it all mean and what can we do to stop this?" Adam sounds as confused as I'm feeling and Elliott shrugs.

"Hand it over to the FBI, I'm guessing. I haven't had much time, but there are some other entries I need to investigate further."

"Like what?" Adam interrupts.

"Flight information, hotel bookings, expenses, to name a few things. I'm guessing we can cross reference some of these dates to establish their movements. For example, there are entries here where the delivery, as they call it, is returned and then there is no trace of them after that. I'm not sure what that means, but I'm guessing they are given new identities or set up somewhere else."

"Or dead." Adam sounds bitter and I know he's thinking about Jenny and Elliott nods as if he casually mentioned the weather. "It's a possibility. I mean, if you give me another twenty-four hours I could investigate that. I also have a few contacts at the CIA who would be interested in this. I could pass it on if you agree."

"Will that make us criminals, and could we be arrested for theft?"

I am so worried about that and Elliott nods. "Potentially, although I'm guessing if they find anything, you would be released in return for your testimony. There's also something else that needs further investigation."

"What?" We both say it at the same time and Elliott's eyes gleam.

"You may like this part. The foundation has been set up in such a way it's considered non-profit making. Catalina Island is listed as a private residence and no money is ever exchanged for a stay there. It's a listed asset, but all the guests recorded are also on the delivery list, so I'm guessing it's just a cover for the business side of things. However–" His eyes gleam. "The most interesting thing is who the beneficiaries are. I'm guessing it's the next generation who will carry on the good work in the future."

He taps on his laptop and turns it around and I say tightly,

"What's this?" The words swim before my eyes as he says casually, "The next in line, I'm guessing."

"But..." Adam looks confused and Elliott grins, obviously loving every second of this. "The dependants of the current owner. All in line to inherit an albatross, or a gold lined future if that's how you want to look at it."

The names make me catch my breath. Nate, Jenny, someone called Harrison and a few other names besides. The one that concerns me the most though is my own name and I say with a catch to my voice, "Why am I on that list?"

Adam turns and the sympathy in his eyes tells me everything I need to know. "I'm sorry, Katrina."

Elliott whistles slowly. "It appears that you are family, Katrina, which can only mean one thing..."

"Either Chester is my father, or Madelaine is my mother."

I feel the walls closing in on me as my life alters, shifting sideways and causing me to stumble. Everything I ever knew has been replaced by the unknown, and now I don't know who I am anymore. Adam and Elliott are speaking, but I don't hear the words. I am numb. A vessel for a mind that has been blown to the heavens. Images of the past few months, years even, are playing through my mind as if I'm about to die and my life is flashing before my eyes. It almost feels I am because the old one is dead now, anyway.

Somehow, the decision is made to hand this over to the authorities. Adam pays Elliott what we owe him in cash, and Elliott promises to use his contacts to deliver a can of worms. In the meantime, we're to sit tight and wait for them to come calling and as we bid Elliott farewell, I am still trying to digest the information I've heard and make sense of it.

Adam is now my hero because he takes charge of a situation I can't handle right now. He makes sure I eat, drink and am occupied. We head to the cinema to watch a movie, but I couldn't even tell you which one. All I can focus on is the fact I don't know who Katrina Darlington is anymore.

∿

IT TAKES three days before we are visited at the motel by two official looking undercover cops. Harvey Broughton and Ava Hardman. We are taken downtown to their offices and are separated like criminals into two interview rooms.

If I was afraid before, I am resigned to it now and if anything, it doesn't matter anyway because it feels as if my life is already over before adulthood even began.

31

They assign me a lawyer and Imogen Harvey is efficient, kind and practical. The perfect person to have beside me when I need her the most. Ava and Harrison sit opposite, and she informs me the interview will be recorded.

"How are you feeling, Katrina?" Ava's empathy reaches across the table, and I welcome it because I have never been more afraid in my life.

"Shocked."

"It's a lot to deal with."

She says kindly, "Just tell us everything that happened since you met Madelaine Covington. Take your time and in your own words. I just want you to know you aren't in any trouble and we just want to get to the root of the problem."

"I'm not in trouble but..."

She smiles. "I guess you're referring to the money and the things you took from the safe. Obviously, that's an offence, along with the theft of a jet ski. However, how can we prosecute you for something that is yours on paper?"

"Mine?"

She nods. Her painted lips stretch into a wicked smile, "You see, Katrina, you are listed as a beneficiary and when you turned eighteen, your name was added as a shareholder."

"But I never signed anything."

I'm confused that I can be given something so huge without my knowledge and Harrison says gruffly, "They don't play by the rules, and forgery is business as usual for them."

He slides a document towards me, and I see my name scrawled in a box. "Is this your signature, Katrina?"

"No." I blink as he slides another document across the table. "And this."

"No. What is it?"

Ava sighs. "It's accepting liability for The Green Valley Foundation. Signing your life away some may call it, but it's taking responsibility for the running of the company."

"Why?"

"Because they need to guarantee the longevity of the business. I have looked deep into this and it's all quite simple. The Green Valley Foundation is a non-profit making charity, after expenses, which are huge by the way. They donate money to various charities across the world, which is admirable until you investigate some of the beneficiaries."

She shakes her head and says bitterly, "Charities owned by fictitious companies all set up with ghosts at the helm."

"Ghosts?"

"People who don't exist. The money is paid into banks in various countries all over the world, in accounts set up supposedly by the people on this list–you included. Your inheritance was always going to revert to the foundation, but with you on board, it looks as if it was there as your contribution, all with no tax implications. They keep the deposits lower in some and higher in others. In Switzerland alone, they have several accounts. Some are in Dubai, and a few are in Monaco. The more legitimate ones are directed to the US and UK and there are even some in Australia and China. A truly global organisation that doesn't attract attention this way."

She sighs and fixes me with a sympathetic look. "This must have come as a shock. I understand you just lost your parents and came to Catalina Island to work for the summer."

"Yes." My eyes burn with tears, and she says sympathetically. "My condolences for your loss. It must have been hard."

"It still is." I brush my tears angrily away and she passes me a tissue. "Can we fetch you a cup of tea?"

I nod, grateful for the kindness she is showing, and she smiles. "I'll arrange it."

The scraping of her chair is the only sound in the room and as she moves to the door, I hear her whisper to someone outside.

They say I'm not in any trouble, but I disagree because it feels as if I'm about to lose my mind and it's a scary place to be.

She returns and sighs heavily. "I have some news that may not help the situation and isn't proven yet, but I think you should know."

I look up sharply and see the sympathy in the agent's eyes as she destroys my life with a simple sentence. "We have reason to believe that your parent's accident was deliberate."

There is a loud noise in my head that drowns out anything else. The room spins and the faces blur as those words cut me apart like individual knives piercing every part of me all at once. Images of my loving parents dance around my mind and I stare into the abyss as she voices what I think I've known deep inside all along.

A sympathetic arm wraps around my shoulders and a cool draft of water held at my lips. I wasn't aware I was even shaking until now and I hear the lawyer say urgently, "She's in shock."

I shiver uncontrollably, and Imogen says kindly, "Drink the water, and inhale deep breaths. Take your time."

I welcome instruction because I have just been cut loose from the one thing keeping me anchored to sanity and as the news sinks in, all I want is answers.

Lifting my eyes to Ava, I say roughly, "What happened?"

"We can wait until…"

"What happened?" I'm more determined now and will demand she answer me, and she must notice that because she says in a calm voice, "At the time of their death, Madelaine Covington was in town. She had a car rental issued under a pseudonym she uses. CCTV footage places her in the vicinity on the same day, at the same time as your parents. Her phone records reveal a call made to them the day before and an entry in her calendar has a meeting set up in town on the day they died." She pauses and then exhales sharply. "Half an hour after they died."

Harrison interrupts. "We believe they were on their way to meet her, and her car was last captured on CCTV, leaving the town on the same road they would have travelled in on."

Ava nods. "The investigation reveals your parent's car swerved before impact. We think they were avoiding something and crashed through the barrier into the embankment below."

"Are you saying you think it was Madelaine?"

"We can't say for sure, but it would explain a few things."

"Then you have nothing."

"Not entirely." Ava taps her fingers on the desk. "We can't prove anything, but a few witnesses came forward and remembered a red car heading their way before they came across the accident. They were surprised the driver hadn't stopped because surely, it's human nature to stop at the scene of an accident, especially one that's just happened. Nothing to implicate her in any way but interesting, don't you think?"

Her eyes light up as she carries on. "We looked deeper and discovered that Madelaine's movements coincided with a few other unexpected deaths over the years. Similar things happened, and a pattern has emerged. In every case, the people who died left a child just after they turned eighteen. That child then disappeared and hasn't been seen since."

There's a pounding in my ears that won't go away and the soft hand of my lawyer rests on my arm as she says coolly, "I think my client could use a break."

"No." I shake my head, saying roughly, "I want to know everything."

Ava nods. "Yes, I would too, in your position. The bare facts are these. This isn't the first we've heard of The Green Valley Foundation. It may surprise you to know we've been gathering evidence for some time. When your friend alerted us to this, it accelerated things a little."

"You knew?"

I stare at her in shock, and she nods. "We are gathering evidence because we need this to be watertight. These people cover their tracks and have explanations for everything. Any potential witnesses are not to be found and we have nothing to charge them with that would stick for long. Sure, we could arrest them on any manner of things and tie them up in red tape for ever, but we want the one thing that will send them to prison for the rest of their lives and we are almost there."

"Can I help?" I push away my shock with just the numb feeling of revenge building inside and Ava nods. "Would you be a witness in a court of law?"

"Definitely."

"Then leave it with us, Katrina. We will bring them in for questioning and present the facts."

"I want to go back."

She half smiles. "I thought you would."

I nod, feeling my nerves being pushed away by anger. "I want to confront them. Look them in the eye and demand answers, and I don't care if you wire me up to get your evidence. I just want to bring them down—for my parents."

32

I don't know how this has happened, but after I made my decision, I set off a series of events that will send me back to Catalina. Adam tried to talk me out of it. He made his own statement and was told he's free to leave. He plans on taking a job in a restaurant the FBI arranged to start him on the right track. He is one of the lucky ones because he can leave with a slate wiped clean in return for acting as a witness, and I know he will be protected.

As we say our goodbyes, I hug him hard and say emotionally, "Thank you for everything."

"I did nothing, Katrina."

"You saved me, Adam. I was seduced by them and wouldn't have left if you hadn't swooped in like a hurricane and taken me along with you. I owe you everything."

"I wish you weren't doing this." He grips me hard, and I'm almost tempted to go with him. He is the only person I've got left, and it's so hard leaving him behind.

"I'll come and visit." I smile with a bravery I don't feel inside, and he seems a little upset as he growls, "If you don't, I'll come and find you and that's a promise."

I smile through my tears. "It will be ok, you know."

"I know." He smiles and says with a sigh. "I wish..."

"I know." Smiling, I back away and take a deep breath. "Wish me luck."

I turn and leave the only friend I have left, and it doesn't make me feel that great. I will miss Adam. He was the only person strong enough to try to break this vicious cycle and I owe him my life; I really believe that.

A car is waiting to take me back to Naples, where I will call the island and ask them to come and fetch me. The driver is a special agent who will brief me on the journey and by the time I get to Catalina, I will know what I must do. In my bag are the folders, flash drives and most of the money. I have my story and a monitoring device secreted behind my ear, hidden in my ponytail. Above all though, I am determined to face the woman who ruined my life and demand the answers I need.

∼

As I stand shivering on the dockside, I make the call and Chester answers, telling me he survived his attack at least–unfortunately.

"Catalina Island."

"Chester, it's Katrina."

There's a short silence before he says casually, "What happened?"

"I'll explain later, please can you come and get me? I'm on the dock in Naples."

"I'll send Nate."

He cuts the call and I start shaking. What am I thinking? I'm not sure I am strong enough for this, and it's only the thought of how scared my parents must have been before they died, hardens my heart and gives me the resolve to see this through.

Twenty minutes is a long time to wait when your life may change forever. I run through everything in my mind and plan on how to play this. I need them to believe me, to feel sorry for me and let me back in and I wrap my arms around my body as if comforting a small child who can't find her parents. That's exactly how it feels to be me. Ever since they died, I've felt so alone. Catalina gave me something I needed and now I know it was all built on lies, I feel the ground shifting, threatening to pull me under. The only thing giving me strength is my desire for answers, and there are only two people who can give me that.

I hear the boat and feel my heart lurch when I see Nate heading my way and I swallow the lump building in my throat because I can't help my feelings for him. Perhaps he's as innocent as I am, and yet I wonder about that when I remember what I've heard. Looking eagerly for his reaction, my heart sinks when he looks guarded, disappointed, angry even. I watch as he pulls alongside and jumps out, securing the line before he turns and says in a sad voice, that throws me a little, "You shouldn't have come back."

Clutching my bag against me like a shield, my voice shakes as I say, "I never wanted to leave in the first place."

He looks surprised. "But I thought..."

"It wasn't me, Nate. I was forced to leave."

He takes a step towards me, and I hate seeing the hope flare in his eyes. "Adam?"

I nod, the tears resurfacing, making him reach for me. As I fall against him, his strong arms wrap around me and for a moment, it feels so good to be in his arms again. He holds me gently and says huskily, "What happened?"

"When you left, Adam arrived, and it was horrible. He had a gun, and he forced me into Chester's study. Then he bound my hands and told me to shut up while he looked for anything valuable. He knew exactly where to look as well, and even knew the code to Chester's safe. I pleaded with him, but I didn't recognise him. He was angry, frightening, a mad man and I thought he would leave me for dead if I didn't go along with him. I was so afraid and when he found the cash, he took it all and then forced me to go with him. He called it his insurance policy."

"Katrina, I'm so sorry."

I rest my face against his chest, feeling my heart thumping because this cover story has to work. I must regain their trust if I'm to survive and so I sob, "I played along when we reached the mainland because I wanted to come back to you and not end up dead somewhere. As soon as I had my chance, I got what I could and escaped and it's taken me so long to get back."

"What happened to Adam?" Nate's voice is laced with controlled fury, and I shrug. "I'm not sure. He could be after me, in fact, he probably is. I'm so frightened, Nate. I kept on looking over my shoulder, expecting him to catch up with me and I was in a strange country and didn't know how to get back. Please don't think I stole from you. I would never do anything to hurt you, or your family."

The fact he grips me tighter and kisses the top of my head makes my heart sag with relief. He believes me; at least I hope he does.

He says gently, "Let's get you home." He helps me carefully onto the boat and unties us from the dockside and I exhale a deep sigh of relief. The first hurdle is over at least, however, the biggest one is yet to jump.

I am so conflicted as I sit nervously waiting to deal with the consequences of my actions. Being here alone with Nate is comforting yet worrying at the same time. When I saw him again, it felt like coming home and I don't want to feel like that. I want to hate him. To hate them all because, surely, he is part of this huge deception. This manipulation of people's lives, or is he just a victim like me? Then there's the possibility we could be related, although given what's happened between us, that's unlikely. I'm still not sure why my name is on that list, but it can't be because I'm a child of theirs. I don't even want to think about that and yet part of me feels as if nothing would shock me now. Even the twisted thought of intimacy with a member of my own family. These people have no morals and care about nothing but money and greed.

Nate throws me a concerned look and as we near Catalina, I feel the nerves building.

"Are they angry?" I feel worried and note how anxious he looks.

"You could say that. They think you planned it along with Adam. They believe he doctored Chester's food and you let him into the bungalow. It took them a while to discover the safe was empty and it gave them more reason to think it was you."

"I never knew any of it. I was just a hostage, really." Part of this is the truth anyway, because I never knew what Adam was planning and I'm relieved at that.

Nate looks worried. "I meant what I said back there, Kat. You really shouldn't have come back."

"Why not?"

"I can't say."

"Yes–" I smile at him reassuringly, "You can, Nate. Please, I really need a friend right now and you're the only one I can trust."

"Then you're a fool." He looks so sad it makes my heart sink because it appears I was wrong about him and destroys any hope I had left.

"Chester and Madelaine…" he sighs. "Well, they're nice enough, but there's a side to them you won't like. They took me in and made me family, but it comes at a price, and I don't want that for you."

"What price?" My heart thumps like a battle cry and he shrugs, looking as if he would rather not say but feels he should.

"I came here two years ago because I discovered Chester was my father. I told you that. It was ok at first and then he began to teach me the business. I'm not saying I agree with what that involves, but they make it seem so honourable it becomes normal after a while. I've seen others struggle to accept the business and they end up worse off for it and I've learnt the easiest way to cope with life in paradise is to do what you're told. I'm still figuring a way out of the mess I'm in, and I don't want this for you."

He turns and cuts the engine and for a moment we are silently bobbing on the waves and then, to my surprise, he cups my face in his hand and the chaotic beauty in his eyes makes my heart break into a million pieces. "I was so relieved when you left – for you. You had found a way out of the madness, and I hoped you'd be safe with Adam. Now I know it was by force, I want to hunt him down and make him pay. But you escaped and now you have a different kind of battle on your hand. Just know

I'm here for you, whatever you hear to contrary because life on Catalina is the survival of the fittest. I want to protect you, Kat, but I can only go so far, so my advice is to listen, and do as you're told, and we will work out a way to escape this madness together."

He leans down and captures my lips in a surprisingly gentle kiss that feels so tender, loving even, and it takes my breath away. Is he putting on an act to win my confidence? It certainly doesn't feel like that and with my whole heart, I want to believe him. I feel so connected to Nate and I'd hate it to be easily broken. He could be my saviour, he could be my downfall. Only time will tell.

33

As we near the dock, we have a welcoming committee and my heart somersaults when I see Chester and Madelaine waiting hand in hand. Nate whispers, "It's ok, I'm right beside you."

Clutching my bag to my chest, I smile nervously and as we pull alongside them, Chester reaches in and offers me a helping hand from the boat.

Madelaine looks wary and I say nervously, "I'm so sorry. I escaped as soon as I could."

"Escaped?" Madelaine looks at me sharply and Nate says quickly, "Katrina has suffered a terrible ordeal. Adam kidnapped her at gunpoint, and she has run from him, all the time fearing that he will follow her and finish the job."

Madelaine shares a look with Chester, and I say in a tremulous voice, "I took this while he was sleeping and ran. I hope it's all there."

Reaching inside my bag, I pull out the folder and leather pouch and then the large wad of dollar bills and see the relief in their eyes. Chester quickly pockets the cash and clutches the rest tightly against him with a thankful look in his eye as Madelaine sighs and pulls me close, stroking my hair like a doting mother, whispering, "Thank you, darling. Thank God you made it back."

I tremble in her arms for many reasons, and I doubt she would believe what is currently running through my mind. Just imagining her being the cause of my parents' death makes me want to scream and end her own miserable life, but I need to be clever about this, so I sag against her and say in a small, weak voice, "I'm just glad I could help. I'll understand if you want me to go, but I owe you so much I couldn't leave without trying to pay you back for your kindness."

Chester speaks up, saying gruffly, "You have done the right thing, Katrina. We always knew you were the perfect fit for life on Catalina and struggled to accept you betrayed us. Come, we'll talk at the house and arrange some food and drink for you. You look exhausted."

They walk on either side of me with Nate behind us and it feels as if I've passed the first test, at least. I know not to underestimate these people, though, because their lives are surrounded by smoke and mirrors, and it takes a brave person to play them at their own game in order to win against them.

We make it back to the bungalow and I look around,

surprised that I made it back here at all. So much has happened since I was last here and yet you wouldn't know it. Madelaine guides me to sit on the comfortable white settee and Nate drops down beside me, placing his arm around my shoulders and pulling me close. Then he surprises me by saying gruffly, "Tell her."

I jerk my head up in surprise and see Madelaine and Chester sharing a look as if deciding between them.

Chester nods and Madelaine smiles sadly. "While we wait for refreshment, we need to come clean."

My ears prick up because surely, it's not going to be this easy.

She sits down opposite me and smiles sadly. "Did Adam tell you what he found in that folder?"

I nod, the tears sparkling in my eyes when I think of the reason I'm here.

"He told me it was concerning The Green Valley Foundation. The one I asked you about. The organisation responsible for stealing my inheritance."

"I'm sorry to tell you this, Katrina..." Her eyes are brimming with sympathy. "But your parents owed the foundation more than they left in their wills."

"For what?" My senses are heightened as I sense the full story looming and Madelaine looks at me with a kind expression.

"Your parents came to me several years ago. I was a young college graduate who had fallen on hard times." She sighs and looks at Chester, who says with a smile, "It's ok, honey; she needs to know."

Brushing a tear from her eye, she says, "I was much like you were. Alone and afraid, but with one added complication. I was pregnant."

I say nothing and just stare at her as if I don't know what she's about to say.

"I confided in your mother, and she offered to help. She told me she would deal with it, but it would require a huge sacrifice on my behalf."

It doesn't sound like my mother, but I keep a blank look on my face as Madelaine says sadly, "They offered to buy my child from me. As you can imagine, I was shocked and then they explained there was an organisation they heard of called The Green Valley Foundation. They would put me in touch with it and they would take care of all the legal stuff. If I went through with my pregnancy, the foundation would reimburse me and make sure I was cared for."

Her lower lip trembles and Chester reaches across and takes her hand, saying gently, "It's ok, honey, now is the right time."

I hold my breath as she looks me directly in the eye and whispers, "You were that child, Katrina. You are the daughter I sold and the only way I would agree to that was because they promised to send you back to me when you were old enough to understand and could make your own decisions."

Nate squeezes my shoulder tightly in a show of solidarity and I expect if anyone knows how I'm feeling, it's him. However, I'm surprised to realise I feel nothing at all but hatred towards this woman who is begging me to understand. It's in her eyes and she thinks it will be so easy to forgive and forget. The moment I met her, I felt as if I knew her from somewhere and now I know why. She's part of me. Shared DNA that I subconsciously recognised the moment we met.

She shakes her head sadly. "On your eighteenth birthday, I flew to England to meet with your parents. I was going to be with them when they explained everything. The trouble is, they never made it because on the way to meet me, they were in the accident that cost them their lives."

I am so angry listening to her because if that was true, why was she driving in the opposite direction at the time? She has obviously thought this out and fabricated the perfect cover story and I hate her more than ever now.

I blink back the tears as she says in a sad voice, "I'm so sorry, my darling, you must hate me."

Chester interrupts, "Give her time, honey." He turns to me and smiles sympathetically. "Think on it. Madelaine wants to be in your life, be the mother to you she always wanted to be. Try to imagine yourself in her position all those years ago. She had nothing, and it was only when your parents gave her a way out of her situation that she survived. She was young, vulnerable, and scared and didn't know what she was agreeing to and as soon as she legally could, she was on that plane heading to your side."

I don't know how I manage it, but I look down and say, "I'll need time to think about this. It's too much."

A sharp knock on the door saves me, and Madelaine jumps up. "That will be Joseph. Come and eat, darling. Take all the time you need, but know we are here for you. We are your family now and want to welcome you home and provide a safe and loving life for you in our family business."

Chester nods to Nate. "Go and let Joseph in, son."

His words jar against my emotions as they try to paint a picture of a happy family. His son and Madelaine's daughter, uniting to follow in their wicked footsteps.

Nate whispers, "Are you ok?"

"I'm not sure."

I'm grateful for his support and wish we were alone. More than anything, I want someone to confide in, but how can I even trust him? It could all be an act to get me on their side.

My mind is scrambled, and I'm standing on quicksand and wonder if it will drag me under because now I'm back, I'm starting to doubt everything. Were my parents so innocent? Did they 'help' Madelaine and set her on this path? Surely, they weren't much older than she was and how did they know about The Green Valley Foundation in the first place?

We take our seats at the table and if I've missed anything about this island, it's the food and despite how sick I'm feeling, I pick at a salad that ordinarily would have me drooling and requesting more. Instead, I take a sip of the cool sparkling wine to gain some courage from somewhere.

Madelaine seems on edge, and I'm not surprised because she has delivered a bombshell this afternoon. Chester takes charge of the conversation and says in his customary deep voice, "Nate knows how you're feeling because we had a similar conversation a couple of years ago. Different circumstances, but it was along the same lines. My story was much the same as Nate's and I was adjusting to finding my father who I thought had died many years ago. You know how things work here and I was partnered with a girl called Rosemary. Despite how careful we were, she became pregnant and threatened to terminate it. Luckily, Grady, my father, stepped in and told her about The Green Valley Foundation and offered to pair her with a suitable family who were looking for a child."

Nate is silent beside me, but I feel his pain from here and wonder why they are speaking so casually about our lives like this.

Chester exhales sharply. "She gave her baby up in return for money and a new life away from the island. I had no say in the matter but like your parents, the ones who adopted Nate had no cash to pay the fee required, so they put up their home as collateral and if they hadn't paid in full by his eighteenth birthday, the house would revert to the holding company, and they would be evicted. The only way to stop that happening was to send their son to Catalina to work off their debt."

I can't believe what I'm hearing, and Nate says quickly, "I don't think…"

Chester's voice is hard with a cruel edge surrounding it and cuts him off with a terse, "She needs to know the facts before we can proceed."

He looks at me with a hard expression. "The truth is, we supply children to childless couples. People with money who have no other choice. In return, they pay us well, everyone is happy, and nobody ever finds out. If they can't pay, it becomes a little messier and their children are sent to repay their debts on their eighteenth birthday unless they have paid in full. Nate has fathered three children himself and has repaid his own family's debts, but as my child, he is now a major shareholder of The Green Valley Foundation. He is now able to take up his position as my successor and make sure the business thrives in the future. Your debt was paid on your parent's death and as Madelaine's daughter, you now also have a major stake in this company, so take a good look around you, Katrina, because this is your inheritance."

Madelaine says quickly, "Join us, Katrina. Work with Nate and let Catalina blossom and make so many childless couples happy. I will teach you everything I know, and you can take over, leaving us to enjoy our retirement and travel. This could be your life knowing you are spreading love to caring people who have no other option. Join us because if you don't..." She shakes her head. "I'm not sure we can help you."

"What do you mean, help me?"

Nate tightens his grip on me as Chester says darkly, "There are no room for passengers in our organisation and we can't help those who choose to leave."

"So, I can leave."

"Of course." Madelaine laughs in disbelief. 'Of course, you can leave, honey, you're not a prisoner here. People leave all the time, isn't that right, Nate?"

Nate nods, looking so miserable I know something is wrong

and Madeleine's voice rips through the tense atmosphere as she says, "I think the last one who decided this life wasn't for her was Jenny. Such a lovely girl too, with such a promising future." She shakes her head. "I wonder where she is now."

The fact Nate looks uncomfortable, and Chester leans back with a slightly disturbing look in his eye, makes me shake inside. I get the message loud and clear. The only way I can refuse their kind offer is to leave, but I may not make it back to mainland.

34

Nate escorts me back to my old room and I can tell he's unhappy. I'm not that ecstatic about things myself and wonder how on earth I'm going to deal with this?

As we part company, he surprises me by pulling me close and holding me tightly, whispering, "Please stay, Katrina. I don't want to lose you."

"Then come with me." I look up at him and watch his eyes cloud with pain. "I can't." He pulls away and sighs. "The longer you stay, the deeper they pull you in. I have done things I'm not proud of just to fit in. To impress my dad, who I thought was someone to look up to. It turns out he's just a wicked soul whose main driving force in life is money. He doesn't care about me, just what I can do for him and for all her charm, Madelaine is no different. They are forcing us together to become mirror images of them and I don't want that for you. Hell, I don't want that for myself, but it's too late for me. That's why I didn't want you to come back. I thought you were free."

I feel bad for him. He has been caught up in something he had no control over and can see no way out. I want to help him so much and yet how can I? I need to make them pay for this and in exposing them, I take Nate down with them.

Impulsively, I nod towards my room. "Stay with me tonight."

He looks surprised. "But…"

"No, please. I don't want to be alone right now, and you're the only person I trust. Nothing more than someone to hold when the world is in chaos around them. Please Nate, let me help you in return for helping me."

He appears touched and I see a sheen of tears glistening in his eyes as he says gruffly, "Thank you."

I grip his hand tightly and lead him into my room because I wasn't pretending. I do want him with me because he is even more of a victim than I am.

As we lie in each other's arms, we whisper in the darkened light about our fears. He confides how much he hates it here, his father and the whole situation. Like me, he was cruelly sent back here while they pretended to help him. When all along it was a carefully orchestrated plan to bring him in line. Our whole lives are one big plot twist and it's up to us to break this cycle.

As we lie side by side, I whisper, "Tell me what you know about the foundation? Is there anyone else involved?"

"There are two more directors who live in Monaco. They

head up the business side of the operation and arrange the fake paperwork and deal with the finances. Chester and Madelaine run the island and the sales side, for want of a better word." He falters and I wonder what's coming next. "There is something you should know before you make your final decision…"

I hitch my breath. "What?"

"Jenny is the daughter of one of the directors."

"She is?"

I hold my breath as he whispers, "She was returned here the same way we were. When Chester told her what was expected, she went crazy. She fought against it and refused to repay her parent's debt. She told Chester to tell her ghost of a father to stick his island because she was leaving and reporting them to the police."

I say absolutely nothing because I can tell he needs to confide in someone and his voice breaks as he whispers, "Chester told me to take Jenny from the island as she wanted to leave."

A feeling of dread is overwhelming me as I lie stiffly beside him, dreading the next words that may fall from his lips. "It was horrible, Kat. He told me I had to make sure she never made it back to the mainland. I was to return alone, and he directed me to the reef where the sharks dine."

"What happened?" My voice is husky and my mouth dry, but I must know, even though he will probably confess to a murder, and my heart thumps as he says in a voice devoid of all emotion. "We argued. She was so angry and told me she was going to make sure nobody ever stepped foot on Catalina again. She would tell everyone she could about what went on here and I knew I had to act to save us all."

"What did you do?" My voice is working but my heart is threatening to give out on me at any second and he sighs, "She was hysterical, so I struck her across the face to calm her down. It worked."

He turns to face me, and I wish he hadn't because even in the darkness I see them sparkle with triumph. "She fell, and it gave me time to increase the speed on the boat and take us out of view. By the time she recovered, we were out of sight and so I told her I had a plan, but she needed to agree to it. Her life depended on it."

"What plan?" This isn't going how I thought it would, and he smiles. "I told her that Chester ordered me to feed her to the sharks. That got her attention, and she fell silent. So, I explained there was a small beach on the other side of the mainland that I could drop her off at and she could call the number of a friend of mine who would help her. In return, she had to lie low and not tell anyone what she had discovered. I would work hard to bring this foundation down, but she had to agree to stand by me when it came to trial, if it ever did."

"But why not let her tell someone? It would all be over by now, surely?"

"No, Kat." He says in an urgent whisper. "They have it all covered. You heard them tell you your own story. They will have thought of everything, and I need to get proof they are selling children."

"Surely the authorities could trace that back; you're putting yourself at risk."

"I'm not." He looks animated as he says, "I have a plan that will bring this madness to an end and make it up to everyone affected."

He laughs softly. "Jenny agreed with my plan and to make it look as if I'd done as Chester said, I caught a fish and gutted it with my knife. If he came to meet me, I would have the bloodied evidence and he would think I had disposed of the problem. I left Jenny on shore and gave her enough money and the number of my friend to help her and returned. I have enlisted help and we are currently gathering evidence, ready to tear this island apart."

"Are you serious?"

I sit up and say in total surprise. "Who?"

He pulls me down and whispers in my ear, "Matty and Diana."

"What?" I stare at him in shock, and he nods. "They're not who you think they are. They are undercover operatives and were sent here to gather evidence. When I confided in them, it all came out and we have been working as a covert team together. Diana is translating conversations that Chester has with the other directors in Monaco. She's fluent in French and the headphones are taped conversations that we have managed to record, courtesy of Matty's skill in security devices. Diana is making notes of the guest's details and sending the information back to Jenny, who is keeping records and acting as our eyes on the mainland. Diana has a phone and a personal VPN that can't be traced. It helps to have friends in high places, which is why I know I'm doing the right thing. Soon we will have enough to take to the authorities and close this island for business and set us all free."

He reaches up and strokes my face with a tenderness that I crave and whispers, "I'll look after you, Katrina. I won't let them hurt you. Trust me, everything will be ok."

As I snuggle in his arms, I want to believe him so badly and I want to trust him. A large part of me does because everything he told me so far has a ring of truth attached and now I know I'm not alone anymore, I drift into a much needed sleep.

35

ONE WEEK LATER

Madelaine is leaving today, and she's not going alone. Their departure was delayed after Chester's attack and mine and Adam's subsequent disappearance. Now they believe it's business as usual. All week Madelaine has schooled me in what's expected. How things run on the island and showered me with affection and compliments. She believes we are building a healthy relationship, which is why she looks so sad as I walk with her to the dock.

"I hate leaving you so soon, darling. I'll try to be quick, but I've already postponed too many meetings."

She sighs and says wistfully, "Maybe you can come with me next time. We can go on a girl's trip, and I'll show you how amazing this life can be."

"Can I?" I sound excited, which shocks me a little because I appear to have settled into my role so easily, I always feel as if I'm playing a part.

There have been many long conversations and cosy evenings discussing the past, the way forward and the future. Chester and Madelaine approve of my accelerating relationship with Nate and believe that the crisis has been averted and its business as usual. I managed to convince them that Adam hadn't done anything with the flash drives and folder and was just interested in the money.

Madelaine told me that she had a private investigator looking for Adam and if he was planning on causing trouble for any of us, he would be dealt with. Thanking God that Adam has the best protection possible; I am worried about the lengths they go to protect their business.

Madelaine stops and says quickly, "Excuse me, darling, I need a word with Chester. Carry on without me."

I see Chester heading our way with a frown on his face and my heart rate increases. Katie is walking beside him, and the situation looks tense, and I wonder if they've had words because he takes Madelaine's arm and leads her back up the beach towards the resort.

I look at Katie in surprise. "What's happening?"

She frowns. "I told him I didn't want to leave, and he had to do the right thing for once. I won't go and stay with the people he's making me give my child to. I want to keep it and make a life with him."

"Katie!"

She sniffs. "I had to try. I know I've just made a bad situation worse, but I can't help how I feel."

"What did he say?"

"That he would talk to Madelaine and see if there was a different solution available. I told him if he didn't help me, then I'd report him to the cops for rape."

"This is bad."

I pull her along with me to the boat where Nate is heaving the cases ready for departure. He looks up and smiles at Katie, but after seeing the look on her face, he throws me an anxious look.

"What's up?"

"Katie said she won't go and unless Chester supports her and allows her to keep the baby, she's telling the cops he raped her."

Katie stares at us defiantly. "I mean it."

Nate looks worried. "Where's Chester now?"

"Telling Madelaine things have changed, I guess."

A cold feeling chills my soul because I know what Nate's thinking and Madelaine is probably being briefed on a scenic route change, via shark reef and Nate has paled under his suntan which tells me he thinks the same.

"What are we going to do? Madelaine will be there." I must sound anxious because Katie says sharply, "What are you talking about?"

She looks suspicious and Nate says urgently, "Katie, tell them you didn't mean it. You'll do as they ask and then you may make it to the mainland."

"I don't understand."

"Please Katie, just do it. You'll be safe then."

She looks worried. "Are you saying I'm not safe now?"

We see Madelaine and Chester heading our way and I say urgently, "Please! Tell him."

As they near the boat, I see the glint in Chester's eye and the frown on Madelaine's face that tells me things aren't looking good for Katie and Madelaine says with a hint of steel in her voice, "Katie, I understand you don't want to leave."

The hard gleam in her eye makes my heart sink and for the longest seconds Katie looks at Nate and then sighs. "I'm sorry. I think I was having a panic attack. I'm good now. Shall we go?"

Chester's eyes narrow and he says roughly, "What's changed?"

She runs her fingers through her hair and sighs. "I suppose now it's happening, I just want to get on with it, so I can return quicker."

She says in a small apologetic voice, "I'm sorry. I think my hormones are all over the place. One minute I'm up, then down. I'm sure I'll be fine when I'm there."

I'm not sure if they believe her or not, but obviously don't want to push it, so Madelaine says lightly, "Then that's settled. We'll head off before it gets dark. It's quite a journey to Texas and we need to get a move on if we're going to make our flight."

She turns and falls into Chester's outstretched arms, and they enjoy a long and leisurely kiss, and I watch Katie's face harden as she looks away.

I notice a strange look passes between them when they part and as Nate helps Katie into the boat, I watch as Chester whispers something to Nate and from the look in his eye, I know exactly what he said.

I don't stop to think and say quickly, "I'm sorry, I really need to use the bathroom. Have a good trip."

Without even waiting to hear their replies, I head off because I only have limited time left to help Katie.

Running back up the beach, I head straight for reception, grateful to see Diana silently listening to her headphones. She straightens up when she sees my face and says in an urgent whisper, "What is it?"

"It's Katie." I pant, "I think they're heading to shark reef."

I don't need to explain further because she turns away and reaches for her bag and heads to a small corner of the room. I watch as she talks softly into the phone and wait anxiously in case Chester comes back and as she cuts the call and moves to my side, she whispers, "Thanks, Katrina. We've got this."

She replaces her headphones and smiles reassuringly, and I'm not sure what I should be doing. Heading to the restroom, I play it safe and cover my tracks and just hope Katie makes it back to the mainland safe and sound.

When Chester returns, I am behind the desk where I belong, and Diana is on her break. He hesitates in front of me and says with concern, "You know I'm here for you, Kat. When Madelaine's away, you can always come to me."

I throw him a beaming smile and nod gratefully. "Thank you, you have all been very kind."

He hesitates and then says with a searching look, "I'm glad you came back. You did the right thing because it proved that you're one of us. Welcome to The Green Valley Foundation, Katrina. You will never regret your decision."

I watch him walk away and feel my heart thumping painfully hard. This is getting serious now and I hope to God Katie makes it.

∼

HALF AN HOUR LATER, I look up as Diana reaches my side and whispers, "Katrina, you must go to your room and stay there."

"Why?"

"I'll explain later. Matty has told the guests we're running a drill, and everyone must head back to their room until they are notified it's clear."

"A drill?"

She grins. "Security breach."

"But."

"Just go to your room, Katrina. It's important."

I watch some of the guests hurrying back to their bungalow and, with a worried nod, I do the same. I feel so anxious and wonder what's going on and as I make my way down the path that leads to my room, I see the boat returning, but it looks as if Nate's not alone.

Rushing quickly inside, I head out onto the balcony and see Nate step out with Madelaine and Katie, and then I see two other boats heading into the dock. It's obvious those figures aren't incoming guests and I hope to God Diana called the cavalry.

The million-dollar question is, what did they see?

36

Approximately two hours later, there's a loud knock on the door and I rush to answer it feeling anxious. This has been the longest two hours of my life, and I see Diana waiting for me with a relieved smile on her face.

"It's ok, you can come out now. I'll explain on the way."

We head off and she whispers, "Thanks to you, I alerted the local police who sent a couple of boats to shark reef. They viewed the whole thing and recorded it."

"What happened?" I'm so worried about that and she says

grimly. "They saw Madelaine punch Katie in the head and take out a knife. She pulled her head back and as she held the knife to her throat, Nate pushed her away and pulled Katie behind him. They argued, which was when the police went in and arrested them. They escorted them back here and then two more boats arrived with FBI agents who were alerted by Matty, and he took them all to Chester's office, where he was busy trying to destroy evidence."

"So, what now?" Part of me thinks they will have a ready-made excuse for that, and Diana grins. "Game over. They were arrested and read their rights and escorted from the island in separate boats. There's a staff meeting now and a separate one for the guests. I'm told the guests will have transportation arranged to take them home after they have been questioned and their statements prepared."

"And Nate?" I'm so worried about him, and Diana grins. "Safe and sound. Nate has been cooperating with us for months and he saved Katie's life. He will be a strong witness for the prosecution, and I'm guessing Chester and Madelaine will be enjoying a different standard of living from now on."

"Prison?"

She nods. "If the authorities can prove they murdered people and trafficked babies, they won't be tasting freedom for quite some time – if ever."

She looks around and shakes her head. "I don't know what will happen to Catalina, but I'm guessing its days are numbered."

"What about the other directors?"

"They were arrested in a coordinated raid. We've been planning this for months but needed to make sure the case was watertight. Katie's evidence will help finish this, and everyone can finally get on with the rest of their lives."

We reach the canteen and the first person I see is Nate, who is sitting with his head in his hands, looking as if he's seen a ghost. I rush across and throw my arms around him and as his close around me, I squeeze him so tightly he probably can't breathe.

"It's ok." He kisses my head and whispers in my ear, "It's done, Kat. We did it."

The tears stream from my eyes and he wipes them away with his fingers, his voice husky as he says, "It's ok. I've got you and we'll face the future together."

The relief at knowing I have someone; a person I can support and will support me, means so much, and as I sit beside him with my hand in his, we listen to Matty as he asks the room to fall silent.

"Guys, listen up." A hush settles over the room amid an air of expectation that everything is about to change. "I'm sorry to say that Catalina Island is now closed for business."

There's a slight murmuring and Matty says grimly, "Chester and Madelaine have been arrested and are currently on their way to the mainland for questioning. For those who don't know already, the island was a front for illegal activities and will be seized by the authorities. You will be asked to make yourselves available for questioning and when you are released, transportation will be arranged for your safe return to the mainland."

"What about our jobs, money…" The questions come fast and loud and I look around me at the devastated faces of my co-workers.

Matty says firmly, "You will all receive the pay you are owed and there's a support officer who will try to set you up with a place to stay and a job."

As the staff voice their concerns, Matty answers them as best he can, but I just feel a tremendous sense of relief.

It's over.

Later that evening, Nate sits with his arm around me as we share a cocktail by the pool with Matty and Diana. The rest of the staff are also sitting in their own groups, enjoying the facilities along with the guests. Everyone is shocked at what's happened but determined to wrap things up here in a professional manner.

The guests are leaving tomorrow and the various officials who constantly arrive on the island have taken charge of the situation, which fills me with relief.

Matty looks at us with concern. "Are you ok?"

Nate nods, increasing the pressure around my shoulders, making me feel safe and no longer alone.

"We'll be fine. I have a friend who can help us who owns a bar in Kissimmee. We'll head there and wait out the storm."

"It could take months, years even. It's such a mess." Diana shakes her head, looking concerned.

"It doesn't matter. We'll be fine." Nate sounds confident about that, and I am so happy he turned out to be the good guy after all. With him beside me I can achieve anything and I'm extremely grateful to his friend who Nate assures me will arrange a work visa for me enabling me to stay and possibly finish my education here.

Diana looks at me a little sheepishly, "I'm sorry we lied to you, Katrina. We had our cover story and had to act the part. No hard feelings about that?"

She looks at me warily and I laugh. "If you ever grow tired of undercover work, you would do well on the stage. In answer to your question though, no, definitely no hard feelings."

Nate turns to Matty, "What about you? What happens now?"

He smiles at Diana. "We'll get another assignment."

"Not until we've had that vacation you keep promising me."

Diana rolls her eyes and Matty grins. "Of course, it's the only thing that's kept me going."

He smiles lovingly at his partner in every way, and I wonder what it's like to be them. Working together in strange circumstances that aren't without risks.

As the sun sets on the most turbulent day of my life, I lean my head on Nate's shoulder and sigh. Despite everything that's happened, I found him, and we will face the future together, for however that lasts.

EPILOGUE
THREE YEARS LATER

The sun is high in the sky and on maximum heat setting – at least it feels that way.

A faint sheen of sweat glistens on my face as I catch sight of myself in the mirror.

"How are you feeling?"

Nate stands beside me, as we share the same reflection, and my heart skips a beat as it always does when I stare at the man I love with my whole heart.

"Nervous, I guess."

"Same."

We share a moment of reflection in more ways than one because today our lives change forever.

"I wish they were here."

I don't need to give them names because Nate knows exactly who I am speaking about.

"They would be so proud of you."

"I know."

The tears glisten in my eyes as I remember my parents, whose only crime was to do everything possible to have their own child.

The trial revealed they weren't the first people who lost their lives, leaving their entire estate to The Green Valley Foundation. In every case, there was proof that a meeting had been set up with Madelaine Covington which they mysteriously never attended. Painstaking investigation and witness statements were collated from around the world, and she was convicted of several counts of murder when she was brought to trial. The backlash was huge, and it was the case of the century. They were soon notorious and the deeper the authorities dug, the more dirt they found. Trading in humans, extortion, murder, and fraud. All under the umbrella of The Green Valley Foundation. Millions of dollars were discovered in accounts all over the world, and the scale of the operation was mind-boggling.

Madelaine and Chester were sentenced to life imprisonment and the only contact both Nate and I had with them was facing them across the crowded courtroom as we gave evidence against them.

The fact they were our mother and father meant nothing. They just gave us life in the first place and gave up any rights to our loyalty the moment they walked away. Madelaine played her part well in the witness box. Looking as if butter wouldn't melt in her mouth and trying to blind the jury with her large contrite eyes and trembling lip. Chester turned on his considerable charm, but the jury saw right through them. Luckily, the evidence was too great, and they lost everything they had spent years trying to protect. The thing I'm most grateful for is that Nate and I are in no way related. My father was a one-night stand in a bar on one of Madelaine's travels. Apparently, she always made the most of her nights away from Chester and was no better than him. They deserved one another and deserve their future, and I hope I never see either of them again.

"We should be leaving."

I brush some more face powder on my nose to disguise the sheen and smile. "I'm looking forward to this."

Nate's hand slips into mine and he spins me to face him and smiles lovingly. "I love you, Katrina Darlington, and can't wait to begin my future with you."

"To do it right this time."

"To make our parents proud and not the ones who gave us life."

"Never them." I smile as we share a special moment before the day turns into chaos. The moment where our world rights itself and sets us on a path of new beginnings.

We walk hand in hand out of the sensational bungalow that we now call home and lock the door behind us, knowing that when we return, our peace will have been shattered.

As we make the short walk down the path that is flanked by sweet-smelling flowers, I sigh with contentment. We made it. This is our life now and we will make it count.

As we head towards the beach, I feel the sun on my face and take in deep, cleansing breaths of the fresh, salty air. Catalina Island has never looked as special as it does in this life changing moment and watching the boat approach, I feel the excitement stirring deep inside.

"They're here."

We watch the boat head into view and Nate squeezes my hand. "Are you ready for this?"

"I've been ready for it my whole life."

As the guests take their first look at paradise, I enjoy watching their awed expressions and excited smiles. Their delighted laughter lightens the atmosphere and brings life to an island that was only ever enjoyed by a privileged few.

When the dust settled on the trial and the four directors were sentenced to life imprisonment, the beneficiaries of the foundation were given control of the only legal parts of it that were left, after paying fees and creditors. Catalina Island was the jewel we inherited, and we set up an island trust and used the money to make it a luxurious holiday resort.

Now our guests are arriving, and Nate and I oversee an island paradise that welcomes paying guests for an idyllic break on their own private island.

The children who lost so much and were forced to work off their parent's debts are all shareholders and it's now run as a business that pays dividends. At least that's the plan if we can make it work, and I'm just grateful that Katie and Jenny have stepped up to sell the dream around the world from the comfort of Catalina. Jenny wasted no time in rekindling things with Adam, who returned as our head chef and Drew is excited to be our bar manager. Katie and Sven talked it through and decided to settle on the island and bring up her child together. We are all desperate to make this work and now have a purpose far more noble that the one we first inherited.

I watch as Nate helps a child down from the boat and his easy smile makes me feel warm inside. We'll be ok. I know in my heart that out of great pain has come the sweetest pleasure. Catalina Island was always my destiny but sometimes destiny is what you make it and if you're not happy with the one fate has dealt you, it's ok to tweak it slightly and make it a better one.

∾

"IT IS NOT in the stars to hold our destiny but in ourselves."
— *William Shakespeare*

∾

IF YOU ENJOYED this story you may be interested in The Resort

MORE BOOKS & ME

Thank you for reading Private Island.

If you have enjoyed the story, I would be so grateful if you could post a review on Amazon. It really helps other readers when deciding what to read and means everything to the Author who wrote it.

Connect with me on Facebook

Check out my website

Thank you

I feel very fortunate that my stories continue to delight my readers. The Girl on Gander Green Lane reached the number 1 spot in Australia in the entire Kindle Store. The Husband Thief and The Woman who Destroyed Christmas reached the top 100 in Canada, the UK and Australia.

I couldn't do it without your support, and I thank every one of you who has supported me.

For those of you who don't know, I also write under another name. S J Crabb.

You will find my books at sjcrabb.com where they all live side by side.

As an Independent Author I take huge pride in my business and if anything, it shows what one individual can achieve if they work hard enough.

I will continue to write stories that I hope you will enjoy, so make sure to follow me on Amazon, or sign up to my Newsletter, or like my Facebook page, so you are informed of any new releases.

With lots of love and thanks.

Sharon xx (M J Hardy)

Ps: M J Hardy is a mash up of my grandmother's names. Mary Jane Crockett & Vera Hardy. I miss you both so much & wish you knew this chapter in my life. One of my fondest memories is sitting in my grandmother's rocking chair by her gas fire, reading her collection of Mills & Boon books when I was about 12 years old. I wonder what she thought of that – I dread to think!

Check out my other books

The Girl on Gander Green Lane

The Husband Thief

Living the Dream

The Woman who Destroyed Christmas

The Grey Woman

Behind the Pretty Pink Door

The Resort

Private Island

You're Invited!

Join my Newsletter

Follow me on Facebook

Printed in Great Britain
by Amazon

43793493R00148